FIRST LOVE

Thirteen-year-old Jessie is a romantic, and she and her friends spend hours talking about LOVE. Spin-the-bottle is considered "practice for the main event" and the ideal boyfriend is Burt Reynolds. But Jessie knows that if she's patient, the *real* thing is bound to happen sooner or later. And it does.

Jessie first spots Michael and his band playing at a shopping mall. When they meet, she is shy and nervous. Michael is handsome, charming—and seventeen. Jessie tells Michael that she is sixteen, sure that he won't be interested in her if she reveals her real age. Jessie is ready for her first love, and much to her surprise, Michael is ready for Jessie.

SOONER OR LATER

BY **BRUCE AND CAROLE HART**

AVON
PUBLISHERS OF BARD, CAMELOT AND DISCUS BOOKS

AVON BOOKS
A division of
The Hearst Corporation
959 Eighth Avenue
New York, New York 10019

Copyright © 1978 by The Laughing Willow Company, Inc.
Published by arrangement with International Creative
Management.
Library of Congress Catalog Card Number: 78-70737
ISBN: 0-380-42978-0

First Avon Printing, December, 1978
Eleventh Printing

AVON TRADEMARK REG. U.S. PAT. OFF. AND IN
OTHER COUNTRIES, MARCA REGISTRADA,
HECHO EN U.S.A.

Printed in the U.S.A.

SOONER OR LATER

One _____

Have you met the Bumblebee?
He is a necessity.
For every flower that you see,
Say thank you to the Bumblebee . . .

Sex education is a joke.

Here I am—my name's Jessie, Jessie Walters, nice to meet you.

Here I am, sitting in this small, dark room with about twenty other kids around the same age as me.

I'm thirteen. I'll be fourteen, this June fourteenth.

Which makes me a Gemini. Which doesn't mean that much to me.

Except it gives me a place to open the newspaper to.

Today is Friday and I'm being super-careful about confiding my plans to an ambitious business associate.

Today is also a warm spring day. The kind that gets you thinking about summer vacation. About beaches and bathing suits and—if you happen to be at a certain age—boys.

I'm at that certain age.

And so are the other girls and boys sitting with me in this small, dark room on this very warm spring day.

All of us are here for the same reason. We are here to learn about sex.

We couldn't have picked a better time.

Or a worse place.

Because the room is a classroom.

An eighth-grade classroom.

In John F. Kennedy Junior High School.

In Englewood.

New Jersey.

U.S.A.

Where sex education is a joke.

They're showing us this film strip—this movie that hardly moves.

It stars this funnypaper bumblebee who wears a yellow-and-black sweater. It seems he's madly in love with funnypaper flowers. Red ones. Green ones. He doesn't care.

As long as they're funnypaper flowers, they're all right with him.

So, this funnypaper bumblebee keeps flying around, spotting funnypaper flowers, diving into them, scarfing up their funnypaper flower nectar and flying off to the next funnypaper flower.

Behind him, the funnypaper bumblebee leaves a trail of *baby* funnypaper flowers.

That's how they teach us about sex, here in the eighth grade at JFK Junior High.

The course is called "The Family, Interpersonal Relations and Human Sexuality."

Our teacher, Ms. Maggie Molloy, is probably an expert on the subject. She went to Columbia, in New York City. She doesn't wear a bra. Once she was married. Now she lives with this guy she's not married to. They say.

But Ms. Molloy's not allowed to say—to tell us about any of that. So she just stands there, at the front of the room, her arms folded across her two breasts, watching the funnypaper bumblebee and his funnypaper flowers. She even manages to look like she's really interested.

It's her job.

But I know it's impossible.

So, I'm reading *Eden in Flames*. Which is perfectly okay because learning about sex is my job, right?

It's terrific.

So, now the moment was upon her! How many nights, tossing, restless in her bed at Three Oaks—how many nights had she dreamed of this moment?

How often had she seen Royal Dalton as she saw him now—kneeling before her, his hand cradling her hand, his eyes searching her eyes, yearning for an answer?

8

"Mrs. Royal Dalton," she thought.

How far she'd come from the tumbled shack on Kelley's Creek.

"Mrs. Royal Dalton—"

"Yes," she whispered.

And suddenly, her eyes burned with tears. And she was in his arms. And he was raining kisses on her hungry mouth.

The sun rose hot over Three Oa—

"I suppose you know all about this stuff, huh?"

Geez, caught in the act.

"No," I tell Maggie Molloy, "I was just—uh—"

But she knows what I was just. I was just reading *Eden in Flames,* when I was supposed to be watching "Thank You to the Bumblebee."

She's not mad. In fact, she's kind of smiling.

But she's not about to let me get away with it, either. She has to keep us in line.

It's her job.

So, she sighs and shakes her head and hits this switch she's got in her hand. And off goes the film-strip projector. And the room is dead quiet for a second. And then everybody's turning around in their seats and peeking through the darkness at me and—

"Let's see the book," she says.

It's under my desk. I had it in my lap, where I thought nobody could see it.

"I'll give it back," she tells me, and then, seeing how everybody's watching, "I just want to see what you've found that's so much more interesting than 'The Family, Interpersonal Relations and Human Sexuality.'"

Of course, that gets a laugh from everybody. Which gives me time to come up with an answer.

"Love?" I say.

"Probably so," she says.

But she won't let me off the hook.

"Let's see it," she says. And she holds out her hand for the book.

Caroline—my best friend, who sits right in front of me —is doing everything she can not to burst out laughing. She knows about *Eden in Flames.* She *warned* me not to read it. She *said* I'd get caught.

9

She wins.

I lose.

I hand the book to Maggie.

She looks at it for a good long time before she says anything. Like she's never seen anything like it. Like it's a souvenir I picked up on my last visit to the moon.

Finally, she says, *"Eden in Flames?"*

She says it like it's the name of some killer disease nobody'd dare give a telethon for.

"There's no love in books like these."

Here it comes.

"There aren't any *people*."

Go ahead, Caroline, laugh. See if I care.

"The people in here aren't anything like real people."

Whack! Maggie starts rolling up the shades, now. Looks like that's all for the funnypaper bumblebee. Looks like Maggie's the star of this show.

"They're dolls! Cutout dolls!!"

Whack! Up goes another shade.

"If it's real love you're looking for—"

Whack! Another patch of darkness bites the dust.

"—you'd be better off watching the adventures of the Bionic Man and the Bionic Woman."

Steve Austin is nothing, compared to Royal Dalton.

"At least they're *partly* flesh and blood."

Caroline's been keeping her eyes on Maggie, whacking her way up to the front of the room. But now, she turns back to me and gives me this sympathetic smile.

"Look, friends," says Maggie, perching on the edge of her desk, "I'm not against sexy books."

Which is probably true.

"Just *bad* sexy books. There are good ones, you know."

She's really serious.

"Maybe you're not quite ready for them yet—for *Lady Chatterley's Lover, Ulysses, Demian* . . ."

Nobody's paying attention to me anymore. They're all watching Maggie. Listening.

"For artists like Lawrence and Joyce, Hesse and Henry Miller—artists, who write honestly and movingly and beautifully about love and life—and sex, as a part of both. Caroline?"

10

"How do you spell 'Chatterley'?" she asks.

It's the way she asks it that cracks everybody up.

Real innocent.

Which is what Caroline is.

"L-A-T-E-R," says Maggie, spelling it out. And that gets a big laugh, too. During which Maggie gets up from her perch on the desk and starts walking back to me.

"As I was saying," she says, all serious again, "even though you're years beyond puppet shows like these—"

She's talking about *Eden in Flames* by Noble Savage, author of *Babylon in Flames*.

"—you're probably not ready for the good books, the books with the human beings, either. But you should know they exist."

She's looking right at me, now. Bearing down on me.

"Good sexy books exist," she says.

Ring!

Saved by the bell.

"Just like good sexy love," she shouts.

Over the bell.

All of us settle back down in our seats.

Me, too.

"If you're patient—"

The halls are crowded with kids. You can hear them. Shouting. Banging lockers. Carrying on. School's out. But not for us.

"—if you don't accept cheap imitations—"

Maggie drops *Eden in Flames* back on my desk. It *does* look kind of tacky.

"—the real thing is bound to come along. Maybe not today or tomorrow, but—please, God—sooner or later."

Everybody breaks up again.

Including Maggie.

Then, suddenly, she looks surprised. Surprised to see us. Sitting here.

"What are you doing here?" she says. As if she didn't know. "Out!" she says. "Everybody out!!"

I laugh and grab my books and head for the door.

Caroline's a step ahead of me.

She looks back, smiles and nods her head toward her notebook. She cracks her notebook open and there's this list:

Lady Chadderlee
Yulisees
Damian

I can't help but laugh.
Neither can Caroline.
We're out the door.
And into the corridor.
And it's all behind us.
And it's all coming up.
Just ahead.
Sooner or later.

Two ————————————————————

It's Saturday in Englewood and there's nothing to do. How we do nothing on a Saturday in Englewood is we go to Hackensack, which isn't *in* Englewood, or go to the shopping mall, which is in Lodi.

It's funny. All week long at school, you just ache to be out and doing something and then, comes the weekend, you're out and there's nothing to do.

I always figure, when I'm at school, that Life is right out there, you know? Walk out the front door and—blam —you're Into It.

Into Life.

Into Love.

But, so far, neither one has showed up.

Maybe they show up on weekdays, during school hours, when I'm busy with funnypaper bumblebees.

Maybe they hang out with Santa Claus and the Tooth Fairy and only show up when I'm asleep.

Maybe they don't show up at all.

But I think they do.

My father and mother are very *alive*. And, so far as I can tell, they're in *love*, too.

With each other.

So, that stuff's out there.

And if I'm not in love, yet, I'm pretty sure I'm going to be. Soon. I've had stirrings.

I know it's weird, but some things get to me.

Some things get to me in a very strange way.

Like Royal Dalton.

When I'm reading *Eden in Flames*, sometimes I *become* Jasmine Bohannon.

13

She's the future Mrs. Royal Dalton. The one from the tumbledown shack on Kelley's Creek.

Sometimes I'm her and I can see Royal Dalton. I can feel his hand in my hand.

We're in this garden where all the trees and shrubs are trimmed and shaped like sculpture, sculpture you can hide behind, lose yourself behind.

There's music coming from inside the house. Classical music. Strings. A quartet.

There's a moon. Just a sliver of a moon. I can see it, reflected in Royal's eyes.

So sensitive. So deep.

Oh, how he wants me.

But do I dare? The rumors! The stories about him! Can they be true?

My heart pounds in my chest.

His hand is hot in mine.

His eyes will not leave mine.

My breath comes hard.

I cannot think.

I must slow down.

I must stop.

I must.

"Yes!"

I hear myself say it.

I'm sure I haven't spoken.

And yet, he's heard it too. Royal Dalton has heard the voice, *my* voice, too.

His eyes shine with joy.

He rises, stands, pulling me up.

Into his arms.

Pressed against him.

"Oh, Royal! Royal!"

His mouth.

My mouth.

Like that.

And it's not just books.

It happens in movies, too.

And sometimes, when I'm listening to records.

Or the radio.

Or just on a bus. I'll be riding along on the bus with somebody—say, Caroline—sitting next to me. And we'll

14

be talking or not talking and just staring out the window.

Suddenly, I'll be gone. My mind, I mean.

My body will be bouncing along Route 4, heading for Hackensack or wherever.

And my mind will be in this Arabian tent or on this white sandy beach in the South Seas or aboard this interplanetary spaceship.

And it won't be alone.

The Arabian Prince speaks no English. But it doesn't matter. Our fate is written in his eyes.

Omar. Oh.

Oh. Omar.

The Pirate speaks no English. But words aren't necessary. It is all there. In the touch of his hand.

Laffite. Ola.

Ola. Laffite.

The Programmer speaks no human language. He is not human. Not in the way that you and I are human. He is not flesh. He is not blood. He has no soul.

Xeron. Yes.

Yes. Xeron.

Then—bang—the bus will hit a pothole. And—wham—I'll be on the bus again.

With Caroline or whoever.

Heading for Hackensack or wherever.

Only my legs will be crossed.

And my foot will be swinging back and forth like a crazy pendulum on an overwound clock.

And I'll feel my legs, my thighs, one on top of the other, rubbing against each other.

And I'll feel—excited.

But I'll pretend I'm not.

Because I'm embarrassed.

It's sex.

I know it.

And it would be a lot less embarrassing if I knew what to do with it. I mean, I *know* what to do with it. But I'd be scared to do anything with it.

Except in an Arabian tent.

Or on a white sandy beach.

Or on an interplanetary spaceship.

15

You don't have to look your mother and father in the eye when you come home from any of those places.

If you did, you'd probably stay right on the bus.

With Caroline.

Heading for Hackensack.

Or Lodi. That's where we're headed now. To the Lodi Shopping Mall. It's how we decided to do nothing this Saturday. Caroline needs a bra.

That's not quite true. She doesn't really need a bra. But I guess she figures wearing a bra will give her unborn breasts something to shoot for.

It's like her breasts are two cars parked in a garage and they won't come out, unless they know there's two parking spaces just waiting for them.

I understand this kind of thinking. I've been through it myself.

For the longest time, I didn't have any breasts at all. When everybody else had little ones, I had none. It got me worried.

Not that there's anything so hot about having a big chest. But there's nothing terrific about not having any chest, either.

So, I worried. And I worried. And whenever I'd take a bath or a shower or just undress, I'd squeeze my arms against my sides in this special way and get whatever I had to pop out a little.

Just so I'd get an idea of what I'd look like, if I ever had breasts.

Just so I'd give my breasts—parked in the garage, just like Caroline's are now—just so I'd give *them* the idea.

They finally got it. Just before the start of school, this year.

After the bathing-suit season.

But just in time for the sweater season.

The lingerie department at Manferd's-in-the-Mall goes on forever. They've got a million contraptions in white and pink and blue and beige and yellow for making more or making less of every single part of your body.

If a person had enough money and enough patience to snap every snap and close every clasp, you could make yourself into a really curvy mummy. No matter what you had to start with.

16

Then you could just sit back and wait for King Tut to send you a love letter.

Caroline isn't so sure she wants to buy a bra, now.

She says it's because there are so many to choose from.

But I think Caroline doesn't want to buy a bra because she's a little embarrassed to get fitted for one.

It gets pretty depressing when you know all you need is a trainer, but you ask for a fitting, anyway. They give you this real tired sympathetic smile that could turn your blood into chalk dust.

I think it's the chalk dust that's got to Caroline. Anyway, it's so long, lingerie department. Hello cosmetics.

Caroline's against cosmetics. She thinks soap and water and sunshine and a good diet are all anybody needs.

They are all Caroline needs. I have to admit it. She's very pretty in a very healthy way.

She's got this long silky blond hair and these big blue eyes and this cute little turned-up nose and a great smile.

Her complexion is terrific, too. Not a zit to be seen, ever. I don't know how she does it.

Myself, I like cosmetics. Not the poisonous ones, of course. Or the ones they make out of coal tar. Or the ones they make out of whales or wild cats. (They really do!)

I like the more organic kind. The herbal ones. The ones with cucumber. And emollients.

Isn't that the nicest word you ever heard?

Emollients.

I don't use makeup, of course. My mother'd have a fit.

But I figure that when my friends start wearing makeup, Mom will give in. She's got her own ideas, but she's not the kind to force them on others, including me.

That's just one of the things I like about her.

Her name's Lois.

My father's named Bob.

She teaches art at the Abraham Lincoln Elementary School.

My dad's an engineer with the county.

There's a lot of things I like about him, too.

I'm pretty lucky that way.

So, here's the lipstick counter. It looks like the world's most expensive crayon box. Except it's only shades of red.

17

Everything from a Baby Pink that's lighter than a baby's lips to blacklist Red that's deeper than a purple rose.

Whatever color you choose, you look like a different person, and all of them are you. Your Baby Pink self. Your Blackest Red self. And all the selves in between.

A woman is standing at the counter. I watch her as she takes this Medium Red lipstick and draws on the back of her hand with it. Then she holds it up to her face and looks into the mirror, trying to see how it goes with her complexion. It goes fine, but not fine enough for her. As she reaches for another lipstick, she sees me watching her. She gives me this kind of smile, like "Aren't you *cute.*"

So, I grab a lipstick. Tulip Red, it's called. And I scrawl it on the back of my hand, just like she did.

This bugs her.

"Excuse me," I say to her very politely. And I move in on the mirror and look into it, holding up my hand to see how Tulip Red goes with my complexion.

I can tell in a second that Tulip Red isn't right for me. And now it won't rub off my hand.

Caroline finds this amusing.

I head for the cold-cream counter. They give free samples. I take a free sample. One, two, three—the lipstick's gone.

Caroline's crushed.

Until she spots the cologne counter across the aisle.

Colognes aren't cosmetics. Not as far as Caroline's concerned. She just *loves* cologne.

So she sprays some on her wrist. Which is okay with me. Then, she sprays some on me.

Which is *war.*

I grab a bottle of cologne and spray her back.

"Hey!"

And the salesperson arrives.

Scowling.

"What do you think you're—?"

"Sorry," says Caroline.

"Sorry," says me.

And me and Caroline waltz away quick. Like we had some pressing business. Elsewhere. Except as soon as our backs are turned, we're giggling. And smelling.

Like lilacs.

And musk.

Not a great combination.

But *strong*.

That's when I spot her. Down the aisle in a separate little corner of the cosmetics department. A makeup artist!

She's got this copper-colored hair and this big red blossom of a mouth. And she's wearing this not-showy-but-rich kind of dress. And these huge pieces of jewelry. And looking like a fairy godmother.

Which I guess she is.

More or less.

"Hey!" I say.

"Huh?" says Caroline.

"Look," I tell her.

And just then, the woman the makeup artist's been working on gets up from the makeup chair. She thanks the makeup artist and starts walking up the aisle, right at us.

Now, I have to admit, I don't know what this woman looked like before she sat down in the makeup chair. But right now, coming at us, passing us, flicking her hair off her shoulders with a quick toss of her head, she looks fabulous!

That does it.

I want to look fabulous, too.

"Come on," I say to Caroline.

"Jessie!" she says. And she gives me her stern look. As if I was about to commit plastic surgery or something.

Caroline knows how I do these split-second things, sometimes. But this one! Getting made up by the makeup artist at Manferd's-in-the-Mall! This one is too much!

"You can't!" she says.

"I'm going."

"I'm staying."

"Good."

"Bye."

We do this all the time. Whenever one of us really wants to do something that the other one of us really doesn't want to do. We split up for a while. Like ten minutes or so. Then we bump into each other again and pick up where we left off. It's democratic, that way.

I semi-charge down the aisle, heading for the empty makeup chair. I don't want anybody to get there before I do. If I have to wait, I know I won't go through with it. And I *want* to go through with it. I want to look fabulous!

Plop—I jump into the chair and spin around to face the makeup artist. She's behind the counter, now—sipping coffee from a cardboard cup, looking out over the rim of the cup, looking all around the store, looking everywhere but right behind her, looking at everyone but me in the makeup chair.

Down comes the cup, down from her red-blossom mouth, down to its hiding place beneath the cash register. Now she turns and—

It's going to be all right!

I think.

The makeup artist looks surprised. But she doesn't look angry. In fact, she's got this funny smile on her face.

She doesn't say anything. She just starts gliding out from behind the counter. Moving toward me. With this funny smile on her face. And her head cocked. First this way. Then that. And her eyes!—big as saucers, sky-blue, and sparkling like jewels in bright sunlight—her eyes sweeping my face, gathering in the highlights and the shadows, as if my face were sculpture in a summer garden.

"How old are you two, anyway?" she says.

Caroline!

She just had to see this.

How old am I?

"If you don't mind," says the makeup artist, "it doesn't make any difference to me. I *sell* the stuff!"

She laughs then. Short but nice. Real nice.

"I believe in it. But I guess you could tell that, hm?"

The red blossom smiles at me and turns to talk with the makeup mirror on the counter.

"Not bad for fifty," says the red blossom to the mirror.

And she turns back to me, laughing.

And she reaches for a bottle on the counter.

20

And smoothing her fingers over my face, she begins making me up.

"Makeup," she says, "it *takes* believing in. . . . Like a magic carpet. . . . It's belief that makes it fly. . . . Otherwise, it's just a rug."

She finishes with the bottle. She takes another and goes to work on my eyes. With my eyes closed, I hear her.

"If you believe in it," she says, "makeup has a magic all its own."

I feel her fingers slip away from my eyelids. I open my eyes. I see her, searching through her assortment of eyeliners. Which one is me?

Blue.

That blue.

Yes.

"Of course," she says, lining my eyes with robin's-egg blue, "makeup is only dime-store magic. . . . But it works, well enough, when it's used properly. . . ."

She's done. She glides away from me. A step. Two. Yes. She's satisfied. She smiles now.

"How old did you say you were?"

"Thirteen," I answer.

"Well," she says, "right now, you look about . . ."

And she grabs the arms of the chair and she spins me around and everything's a blur for a second, and then— bang!

"Sixteen!" she says.

It's hard to admit this without sounding vain. But the me I see in the makeup artist's mirror *knocks me out!*

It's not the usual pretty-on-her-good-days me, the pretty-from-the-right-angle me or the pretty-in-the-right-light me.

It is the beautiful me.

I look fabulous!

And sixteen!

It feels fantastic—looking into a mirror and seeing the person I'm going to be two years from now, looking out at me, looking into me, looking deep, deep, deep into my eyes.

The only time I remember feeling anything like this is—

Once, I was in a forest—a state park, actually—with

21

my father. We were playing Indian, trying to move through the woods fast and without making a sound.

It's real hard to do, because of all the twigs and the dry leaves and your own breath but if you get into it, you can be an Indian.

Almost.

My father's really good at Indian.

Because he invented it.

Except for the Indians, of course.

Or so he says.

Anyway.

I feel my father's hand on my shoulder. Not his whole hand. Just like the tips of three fingers. Very light. It's a signal.

Right away, I freeze.

If we've been good Indians, whatever it is that my father's spotted will not have spotted us. Yet.

There!

Almost close enough to touch!

Two wild deer!

One deer is munching the long green grass that grows at the base of a giant, ancient tree. She's the doe.

Standing next to her, shoulder to shoulder, is the stag. He is not eating. He is the lookout.

Has he heard us?

No.

Not quite.

He thinks he may have heard something, though.

His head is raised.

His ears are pricked.

Except for his nose, twitching, scenting the air, he stands perfectly still.

Then—fastasthat—his head sweeps around and his eyes lock on mine.

And my eyes lock on his.

In the space of time between two heartbeats—

We look deep into each other's eyes.

We recognize each other.

We trust each other.

We are friends.

We wish each other well.

Then—fastasthat—they bound away.

Both deer.

Gone in a single bound.

Into the trees.

Moving.

Fast.

Through the forest.

Without a sound.

Without a sound, my father and I turn to each other. Our eyes meet.

We smile at each other. Then we both turn together and move off into the woods. Moving fast. Trying not to make a sound.

We never talk about it.

About the wild deer and me.

We don't have to.

We're Indians.

That's the only thing I can think of that felt anything like this.

Of course, it's not the same.

I'm not looking into the eyes of a wild deer now.

I am looking into the eyes of the woman I'll be two years from now.

And, like I said, it knocks me out!

"Jessie!" says Caroline, really impressed.

And that almost snaps me out of it.

"You look about sixteen," says the makeup artist. And then she hits me with a bucket of cold water. "But remember, dear—you are *not!* Here's your change."

I've bought a beginner's makeup kit from her.

I owe Caroline $3.75. I remind her to remind me. I'm terrible about owing people.

Or their owing me.

"For when you're ready to be thirteen again," says the makeup artist, dropping a free jar of cold cream into Manferd's adorable little mini-shopping bag.

"Oh," I tell her, and I mean it, "I don't think I'll ever be ready for that!"

Caroline disapproves.

"Oh," says the makeup artist, "I think you will. I know *I* am!"

Which strikes me funny.

And her.

23

And Caroline.

We laugh together and I say thank you and she says thank you and Caroline and me go racing off for the door.

And I can hear music, as I move down the aisle.

Music for flying by.

Because I'm flying.

And I catch myself in a mirror.

And I hear applause.

Like I'm Miss America, snuffling back my tears and putting on that prize-winning smile and promenading the runway at Atlantic City.

And I'm out the door.

Into the shopping mall.

And there *is* applause!

Except it's not for me.

It's for them.

For him!

Three _____

Hear the music.
Let it lift you off the floor,
Till there's nothin' but the music, anymore.
Forget about the world outside the door.
It's better than it's ever been before . . .

"How y'doin', everybody?"

His voice booms through the big amplifiers, stacked on top of the makeshift bandstand, planted smack in the middle of the shopping mall.

The crowd answers him with applause. And cheers. And whistles. They're doin' fine. Super-fine!

I look at Caroline and she looks at me and it looks like we're doin' super-fine, too.

"All right!" I say.

"Yeah!" she answers.

And we take off, full speed, heading for the bandstand.

"Good. Good," he says. "Before we go any further, I want to welcome you all to the shopping mall and tell you, uh . . ."

His voice breaks off, and I can't tell you why, because me and Caroline have thrown ourselves into the crowd by now, and we're twisting and squeezing through the crowd, trying to get up front, so we can see.

"We're appearing here, today, through the courtesy of the mall's participating merchants . . ."

He's reading it. You can tell 'cause his voice isn't comfortable and easy like it was before. He's reading the names of the participating merchants and I'm doing

" 'Scuse me" and "sorry" and picking the holes and shaking my way to daylight.

"Who *are* you?" somebody shouts to the guy with the microphone.

"Oh, yeah," says the guy, breaking off the list of participating you-know-whats. "We're the Skye Band. That's Leroy and Emily and Lenny and Arnie and Mark and, and the rest of the participating merchants are—"

I've almost made it. From where I am, I can almost reach out and touch the bandstand.

"Who are *you?*" the same voice shouts.

And the guy with the microphone laughs at himself for forgetting.

And I bust through to the front of the crowd.

And he sees me.

And, like he was introducing himself to me, he says, "I'm Michael Skye, and this is better than it's ever been before."

And then he turns to the band and starts counting, "One, two . . ."

And I turn to see if Caroline's with me. If she's *seen.* But she's just arriving.

So, she doesn't know.

About me and Michael.

It's our secret.

"And!" says Michael and his voice drops out and in its place, there is the band, a wave of sound, rolling over us.

And *we're* a wave of sound, applause and cheers and hoots and handclaps, rolling over them.

And the two waves of sound meet somewhere high over our heads and crash against each other and recede. And right there, from the deep trench between the two retreating waves, Michael's voice rises.

I wanna' take y'—take y' home with me.
And when I show y'—how it's supposed to be,
You'll close your eyes and grin.
You'll know the place you're in,
It's better than it's ever been before . . .

It isn't just that he's at least six feet tall and lean and

strong and has this lion's mane of dirty-blond hair that reaches down almost to his shoulders.

It isn't just his smile that starts real slow and shy and gets bolder and bolder, as it spreads across his face.

It isn't just his blue eyes, looking right through you, dancing with mischief.

It isn't even his voice, changing moment by moment, rough and pretty, hard and soft, funny and sincere.

Or the way he throws his whole body into the song, dancing the rhythm as much as he sings the words and music.

You can't break Michael down that way.

He's everything at once and something more.

No two ways about it.

Michael is a star.

Not that I'm a great judge of talent.

Or the crowd that's going crazy all around me is a great judge of talent.

We only know what we like.

We *love* Michael.

I can tell by the way y' look—y' never been nowhere.
But gimme a chance to cook—and I'll take you
    there.
To where you've never been.
You'll know the moment we begin,
It's better than it's ever been before . . .

I'm dancing. I didn't *decide* to dance. The music decided it for me. For all of us. Everybody's dancing. Dancing with Michael.

And Michael's dancing with *us*—bounding, prancing, spinning, dropping down, rising up, now close, now far away.

And he starts moving toward me.

Singing.

> *Hear the music.*
> *Let it lift you off the floor . . .*

Singing to *me*.

27

Till there's nothin' but the music, anymore.
Forget about the world outside the door.
It's better than it's ever been before . . .

Just *me*.

I studied life on the street—if you know what I mean.
I wasn't all that sweet—when I was sweet sixteen . . .
But you, you're something else.
You just smile at me, and I tell myself,
It's better than it's ever been . . .

Running fast and silent through a forest.

                Better than it's ever been . . .

Finger tips light on my shoulder.

                Better than it's ever been . . .

The stag stands stone-still.

                Better than it's ever been . . .

Deep, deep, deep into his eyes.

                Better than it's ever been before.

Four _____

Is this love?

I have to ask myself.

If suddenly I can't tell the difference between this guy, singing and dancing in the Lodi Mall, and Omar, parking his camel and pulling back the flap of my tent, does that mean I'm in love?

Of course not.

I'm starstruck.

This is how stars are *supposed* to make you feel.

They're just not supposed to sneak up on you some Saturday afternoon in a shopping mall in Lodi, New Jersey, that's all.

The way it's supposed to go, if you're going to see a star and get starstruck is, first, you have to hassle your folks for a "little extra money this week."

And convince them that rock-and-roll music is an important part of your cultural environment.

And it *is* Saturday night, and wouldn't they like to be off-duty themselves?

The way you usually see a star and get starstruck is you hurry down to your local computer terminal and you get your tickets.

And then, comes the day of the concert, you start early because you're turning your body over to the bus lines.

And the closer you get to the basketball court you're going to, the more people you see who are obviously going there, too—to see the star, to get starstruck.

And then you're there and you're part of this star-hungry throng.

And it takes forever to set up.

And, finally, the opening band comes out and everybody wonders, "Is this him?"

And after about forty minutes, you're pretty sure this *isn't* him, because the crowd is yelling and stomping and hand-clapping and generally drowning out the opening band's third encore.

And then, finally, it's him.

The star.

And he knocks you out.

And he gets you *starstruck*.

It's not love.

I tell myself.

I also tell Caroline.

This is after dinner, that same night, Saturday.

Caroline is staying over.

My folks are out. They go out most Saturday nights. Sometimes they go into the city and see a show or a concert. Sometimes they just go out to dinner somewhere. Tonight they've gone over to their friends, the Fergusons, for dinner and a game of poker.

Grandma is home with us. That's usually where you can find her. Except on her seventy-fifth birthday, which was three months ago, she surprised everybody. She went on a trip to Israel. By herself.

Before she left, I was getting more than a little impatient with her. She was always after me. Jessie this, and Jessie that.

Little things, like "Jessie, put the light on when you read. You'll hurt your eyes."

Just when Babylon is going up in flames but the two lovers, slave and mistress, are too busy making love to notice.

Or "Jessie, don't play your radio so loud. You'll hurt your ears."

Just when Mick Jagger is screeching to a climax on "Miss You."

But she came home different. Stronger, for sure. Walking straighter. Smiling more. She had a wonderful trip, she said. She found her Homeland. Now she's happy. Complete, she says.

And it must be so. Because she's not after me anymore. And it's fun to be with her.

Especially this Saturday night.

Caroline got into asking her a lot of questions about her trip to Israel. At first I thought Caroline was just being polite, but when she'd asked her twenty-first question, I guessed she wasn't, and I started paying attention, too. And it *was* interesting. So interesting that we didn't go up to my room until after eleven-thirty.

At which time I find myself sitting up on the bed, playing my guitar.

Well, teaching myself to play guitar.

They say it sounds terrible for the first couple of years, and you just have to hang with it.

I am hanging with it.

It's been a month now.

But Caroline can't take another second.

"Are you ready?" she says.

She's standing at the door, in her pajamas, and she's got her hand on the light switch and this look like she just drank sour milk on her face.

It's my playing.

And she switches off the light.

And I keep playing.

'Cause you've got to do twenty minutes a day, if you ever hope to get any good at it.

And Caroline jumps into bed. She's athletic, Caroline. And after I whack out a few more chordlike things, she says, "So you thought he was terrific, huh?"

"Who?" I ask her. I know who she means, but I'm not giving anything away.

"The Skye Band guy," she says. And she's teasing me. I can tell.

"Yeah," I tell her, like I'm not all that impressed, "pretty."

She buys it.

I strum.

"Jessie, did you ever really kiss someone?"

"What do you mean, really kiss?" I ask her.

"I mean, so you felt . . ."

Caroline can't find the words.

"You know," she says.

"As if you felt the ground dropping away beneath you?" I ask her. "And you're suspended? Lifted? Arms

31

outstretched? Floating in a softly pulsing sea of Golden Light?"

"Yeah!" she says.

"Nope," I tell her. "You?"

"Kind of," she says.

This is hard to believe.

I mean, if you knew Caroline. That Caroline's "kind of" been "really" kissed! Well, it's very hard to believe.

"Who was it?" I ask her.

"You won't tell?"

"Of course not."

"Dr. Donnie Alexander," she sighs.

"Your doctor?"

"My dentist."

"You kissed your dentist?"

"Not with my *lips!*"

Oh.

Sometimes it's best to just let things go. This seems like one of those times.

"Kissing isn't just with your lips," Caroline explains. "It's touching. And feeling . . ."

"The Golden Light?" I suggest.

"Yeah," Caroline sighs.

I have to ask.

"How *did* you kiss Dr. Donnie?"

"Well," says Caroline, "you know, when they're working on you? And they're leaning against the arm of the chair?"

It begins to dawn on me.

"You kissed him . . . with your arm?"

"Yeah."

"And he kissed you back . . . ?"

"With his hip," she sighs.

"How do you know it wasn't just an accident?" I ask Caroline. "Or just plain leaning? I mean, how do you know Dr. Donnie's hip was kissing your arm back?"

"You can tell," says Caroline.

"The Golden Light?"

"Yeah."

I strum.

"Jessie?"

"Yeah?"

"Maybe you should get another guitar teacher."

"I'm teaching *myself*," I tell her.

"Yeah, I know," she says. Then, "Maybe you should get another guitar teacher."

Which stops my strumming.

And makes me laugh, because it's true. I really should.

"I've been thinking about it."

"Good," says Caroline.

And she scrunches down under the covers.

"Goodnight, Jessie," says Caroline.

"Goodnight, Caroline."

And I switch off the light.

And I lie there.

Thinking.

"Which arm?" I ask.

"Right," she says.

"Nice," I say.

Goodnight, Michael.

Whoever you are.

Five _____

It's Sunday, after breakfast—which everyone makes for herself around our house on Sundays, so you can get up whenever you want to and Mom doesn't have to spend all day making breakfast for everybody.

Caroline ate this disgustingly hearty breakfast and, after reminding me of my promise never to tell anyone about her and Dr. Donnie, took off for her riding lesson.

She goes every Sunday. If they ever get around to outlawing automobiles, Caroline will be in great shape.

Actually, it's for horse shows. Caroline's real good. And looks great, of course. She's won ribbons.

Mom has decided she's not getting dressed today. It's after noon and she's still in her bathrobe. At the moment, she's busy repotting a plant.

She's got all her different dirts and pebbles out, and she's getting this big old clay pot decorated for its latest tenant—an avocado tree that Mom coaxed out of an avocado seed she found inside a supermarket avocado that went into a salad we ate a long time ago. She's also listening to the radio, an Italian opera from New York. And humming along with it.

She's got the same expression on her face she has when she's painting.

Half smiling.

Half concentrating.

My father is listening to the ball game on TV. That's right, listening. When the tube burned out a couple of months ago, he decided he liked it that way— with no picture and just the sound. I thought it was a joke at first. But it wasn't. And now I'm just as glad.

I kind of like listening to TV, too. It sets you free to do other things.

Like what my father's doing right now, while he's listening to the ball game. The County Highway Department is going to build this garage for their snowplows and stuff. They haven't got much money, so it's not going to be a very fancy garage. In fact, it's going to be a very plain garage.

My father's decided that the best thing to do with the garage is to hide it behind trees and bushes and flowers in a kind of park. But, of course, there isn't enough money for a park, either.

So what my father's doing is sitting at his drawing board and trying to figure out how to make a park out of the trees and bushes and wild flowers that are already growing on the lot where they're going to build this plain garage.

And drinking a Bloody Mary.

Which he does every Sunday.

And listening to the ball game on TV.

Grandma's out in back.

In her garden.

It's a vegetable garden. It's her way of contributing. She started it right after she came back from Israel. She also likes to dig her hands into the dirt. It's good for her arthritis.

Which leaves me.

I am bored.

I have eaten, showered, dressed and read the paper.

According to the paper, conditions are favorable for initiating new projects.

I'm going into Hackensack to take a guitar lesson.

You can do that on Sunday in Hackensack, and, Caroline's right, I *should* get another guitar teacher. I mean, how can I teach myself how to play guitar, when I don't know how to play guitar in the first place?

Hackensack is the closest thing we've got to a downtown around Englewood. It was actually a city, once. About a hundred years ago. They made textiles and imported people from Europe and built fine houses and died and took the city with them. The buildings are still there, though. But they're real old and crumbling.

Still, Hackensack's the place to go if you're looking for city-type things like pedestrians and soda fountains and record shops and guitar lessons on Sunday.

The Eddie Nova Guitar Institute is on the second floor of this old marble bank building on Fulton Street. They advertise on the radio. They're open seven days a week and have lessons for beginners and advanced.

The man behind the desk has to be Eddie Nova himself. He's about fifty or sixty and he's wearing this double-breasted suit with big padded shoulders and this real wide silk tie.

"What can I do for you, sweetheart?" he says, as soon as I open the door.

He used to play with the big bands, once. But then he retired back to Hackensack. I guess it was his hometown, because I couldn't imagine anybody picking out Hackensack as a place to retire to. Not when there's places like Phoenix and Tahiti to retire to.

"I want to learn to play guitar," I tell him.

This doesn't surprise him.

"What kind of guitar do you want to learn to play, honey?" he says.

I don't know. I lift my guitar case. It weighs a ton. I lay it on top of his desk and open it.

"*This* kind," I tell him.

He looks at it and then he looks at me.

"I mean what kind of music do you want to learn to play on your guitar, sweetheart? Flamenco? Jazz? Classical? Folk? Rock?"

"The last two," I tell him.

"Uh huh," he says. "And when do you want to start?"

"Now?" I say.

"Figures," he says. And he scrapes his chair back from the desk and hauls himself up onto his feet. "I'll check and see what's available," he says. "You wait right here, okay?"

He lets himself out a door that leads out of his office and down this long corridor where the practice rooms are. You can hear all kinds of guitar music coming from those rooms, all jumbled up together.

I take a look at the bulletin board, just to pass the time. There's people looking for rides to Denver and Los

37

Angeles/San Francisco. There's guitars and amps for sale. Somebody's forming a punk-rock museum and looking for authentic Johnny Rotten safety pins and stuff.

"Okay, sweetheart, third door on your right. It's ten dollars for one hour."

I pay Eddie the ten dollars. It's all I've got but bus fare home.

I walk down this long dark corridor with the jumbled guitar music pouring into it.

I get to the third door on my right.

I can hear someone playing a guitar inside. It sounds so pretty. It's a shame to knock and interrupt.

But I take a deep breath.

I knock.

"It's open," says a voice from inside the door. My knock hasn't interrupted his playing. He plays on as I open the door.

The sunlight is almost blinding. It pours through a big halfmoon window that stretches from wall to wall and ceiling to floor. I squint my eyes and see diamonds dancing in the rays of sunlight.

The music—the guitar music—continues, soft and sweet and, somehow, lonely and far away.

The rays of sunlight bend around his body as he stands facing the window, his back to me, strumming his guitar.

He stops strumming now.

He turns to me.

I'm still standing in the doorway.

"Hiya," he says.

Like a bolt of lightning, illuminating the dark corners of her soul . . .

"Come on in," he says.

And he starts walking toward me.

"I'm Michael Skye," he says, smiling and holding out his hand to me.

"Nice," I say, taking his hand and shaking it.

"To *meet* you, I mean."

And shaking it.

"Me, too," he says.

And he looks down at my hand, still shaking his hand.

And he smiles.

38

"Well," he says, "let's get started, okay?"

I am starstruck.

I am not in love.

I tell myself.

But I do not believe me!

Because I am a total quivering jellyfish!

Because, as incredible as Michael was, singing and dancing and bouncing around that stage at the shopping mall, he's that much more incredible, standing perfectly still, perfectly in front of me, in this perfectly little room with the dancing diamonds in the air.

He wants to hear me play.

Play? I can't breathe!

I play.

With jellyfish fingers, I play.

I play the two chords I taught myself from my teach-yourself-to-play-the-guitar-while-getting-ripped-off-for-three-dollars-and-seventy-five-cents book.

If these two chords had mothers, even *they* wouldn't recognize them.

That's how bad I play.

I cannot look at . . .

I can't even say his name!

He's sitting in a chair a couple of feet away, listening to me play.

He's not in his chair. He's behind me. He's got my wrist—my strumming wrist—in his hand.

"Just relax," he says.

"Relax your wrist and your body and, mostly, your mind. You're not auditioning for a job with the Rolling Stones here, you know?"

It's a joke.

"Just relax and enjoy yourself."

Sure.

"Here," he says, and he leans over my shoulder.

And I can feel his chest against my back.

He leans over my shoulder and starts strumming my guitar.

And I can feel his hair, brushing against my cheek.

And I can smell his shaving lotion.

And I can feel his breath on my ear.

"Now, let me try the fingering," he says, and he reaches

39

his other arm around me and places his hand on the neck of my guitar.

A total quivering jellyfish!

"Just relax," he says.

I take a deep breath.

The music sounds pretty, now.

I turn to look at—to look at Michael.

There. I can say his name.

I can look at him, too.

I can be in his arms and—

"Watch my left hand," he says.

As long as he doesn't look me right in the eye, like that. And talk to me.

"Your turn," he says. And he drops his hand from the neck of my guitar. And he lets go of my wrist. And he stands up straight, behind me. But he doesn't move away.

E major 7th.

E major 7th.

A major 7th.

A major 7th.

I'm doing it!

E major 7th.

E major 7th.

It's not bad.

A major 7th.

A major 7th.

Not half bad.

Not great, but.

Michael's back in his chair.

I owe him a smile.

Me, too.

E major 7th.

A major 7th.

Michael.

Twang!

I hit a clinker.

Wouldn't you know?

But Michael laughs.

A really good-natured laugh.

"You were doin' all right there till you hit the bump," he says, standing up, up, up out of his chair.

Now, he's walking toward me. God, he's tall!

I tell him, "Yeah," but I'm pretty embarrassed. About the clinker. And being such a jellyfish. And everything.

"You'll pick it up," he says.

"You think so?"

"Sure," he says. Like he's really sure.

Hey, I think. Maybe I will.

And he lifts my guitar out of my hands and begins strumming it, without thinking much about it, but playing it as easy as the wind, playing over a field of grain.

"I mean," he says, "I wouldn't go quitting school or anything."

"You think I could ever be as good as you?" I ask him.

"Oh," he says, "I'm not all that good."

"Yes, you are!" I tell him.

He laughs.

"How would you know?" he asks me.

"Uh . . ." I begin, not knowing where I'm headed. Do I admit I saw him at the shopping mall? And give him a chance to admit he doesn't remember seeing me at the shopping mall?

"You can . . . uh . . ." I continue, wondering just what it is you can. Maybe he does remember me, only he doesn't want everything that happened between us back then getting into the way of what we could have, now. It's *possible*.

"You can just tell," I conclude, not all that convincingly.

He's not convinced.

But lets me off the hook.

"Well, I can just tell, too," he says, "about you. You'll do okay, if you keep at it."

"Oh, I will," I tell him. "Definitely."

And he smiles.

Like he finds me charming!

Imagine!

Six ─────────────────────────────

I couldn't wait till Monday. To tell Caroline. But I did.

I could have told her on the phone Sunday night, but then I wouldn't have seen her face. I wanted to see her face. That's the best part.

I waited till first period. We have woodshop together. We're making bookends, which are turning out pretty ugly.

You get a lot of time to gossip in woodshop, because there aren't enough electric drills and saws and things to go around. So you mostly figure out what you're supposed to do and then stand in line, waiting to do it.

So, Caroline and I are standing in line waiting to use the electric drill and I can tell we're going to have quite a wait, because Herman's got the drill and he's checking and double-checking and triple-checking everything.

Because he's got to get it right.

Herman is failing woodshop.

So, while we're waiting in line, hanging onto our half-finished but already plenty ugly bookends, I just casually drop it on Caroline.

How I decided to take her advice and get myself another guitar teacher.

"Oh, good," she says.

How I took the bus in to Hackensack, Sunday afternoon, and took a lesson.

"So soon?" she says.

From Michael.

"Michael?"

Michael Skye.

It takes a second or two to sink in. But then it does.

I can almost see the exclamation point, flashing in the balloon over her head.

"Jessie!" she shrieks, louder than the ripsaw tearing through somebody's two-by-four on the far side of the room.

Heads whip around.

"Shh!" I tell her. I don't want the world to know.

"What happened?" she wants to know.

So I tell her.

"And he didn't recognize you?" she asks, looking stricken, but going right to the heart of the matter.

I can't decide if I should tell her how he might have recognized me but pretended he didn't, because of how he wanted to put the past behind us and start fresh.

About the time I decide to give this explanation a try, Caroline comes riding to the rescue.

"Because you weren't wearing makeup!" she says. "Like the first time!"

Of course!

Why didn't *I* think of that?

The first time, I looked sixteen!

"Yeah," I tell her, and although I'm relieved because I finally understand what went wrong, I say it kind of sad because we're talking about a chance I missed.

"Maybe I will, next time," I tell Caroline, trying hard to sound casual.

"How old is he?" Caroline wants to know.

The truth is, I don't know.

Michael's older than me.

But I don't think he's too much older.

"I don't know," I say, as if it didn't matter.

"You don't know?"

You'd think that was the first thing you're supposed to ask a person!

"I didn't count his teeth!" I tell Caroline.

She is not amused. How old people are is not something to be taken lightly.

She squints her eyes and, just for emphasis, puts on this real edgy voice.

"You'd better be careful!" she tells me.

I swear, you'd think she was my mother or something.

"Older boys aren't like younger boys," she says, getting edgier by the second.

"They're like *men*. Only *younger*," she says.

I get the point.

The point is—almost all the boys my own age don't know all that much about sex and stuff.

I mean, they know in general.

And they're interested.

But they don't, most of them, know exactly what it is they're interested in.

Older boys—like men—know *exactly* what they're interested in.

Because of this, older boys (like men) are harder to deal with.

"Hey, Herman!" I shout.

At Herman, of course.

I don't really know what to say to Caroline.

I mean, I'm not going to ask Michael his age.

And I'm not going to stop taking lessons from Michael because I don't know his age.

So what can I say?

Except what I said.

To Herman.

Who's been hogging the electric drill forever! Preventing me from completing my work on the world's ugliest set of bookends.

So, Herman looks up from this block of wood that he hasn't even begun to drill.

"Hi," he says, smiling his wimpy smile.

"You are not," I tell him, "you are *not* auditioning for a job with the Rolling Stones, you know?"

"Hi, Caroline," he says, giving her the same wimpy smile he gave me.

"How about it?" says Caroline.

"Oh," says Herman, finally getting it. "I was just aligning," he says.

"We were just *awaiting,"* I tell him.

"It's ready now," he says.

"Good," says Caroline.

"Grief," I say.

And Herman gets to work on his block of wood.

And me and Caroline get to work, pretending that neither of us is thinking about Michael.

And what it is older boys are interested in.

Seven ───────────────

My next lesson is Friday. After school.

I'm going to wear makeup.

I'm also going to wear the same clothes I wore that day, at the shopping mall.

The first time!

I'm also going to play the guitar so terrifically that Michael won't believe it.

I'm practicing.

Just the two chords Michael taught me.

I know it sounds simple. But it isn't because you've got to get all of your fingers to hit very particular spots on the strings, which means getting your fingers into these positions that fingers were never meant to be in.

And that's not all.

Once you've got your fingers in one ridiculous position, pressing down all the strings at all the particular places, you've got to switch them—fast as lightning—into another, equally ridiculous position, pressing down the same strings at a bunch of *totally different* particular places.

It's so hard, it actually hurts!

You get blisters.

And cramps in your fingers.

And angry looks from everybody in the general vicinity.

Except Grandma.

Who, I have to admit, is a little hard of hearing.

Lois and Bob—my mother and father—aren't hard of hearing, though. Not even a little bit.

So, they're doing their best to put up with it. With me and my guitar.

I took tap-dancing, for a while.
They ignored that.
It went away.
I was into punk rock.
For about three days.
They ignored it.
It went away.
So now, they probably figure, it's the guitar.
If they ignore it.
It will probably go away.
Except I don't think so.
I practice every chance I get.
Which is quite a lot.
Just the two chords.
They're all I know.

The only good part for Lois and Bob is that the two chords almost never sound the same. Not the way I play them.

The bad part is that they almost never sound good.

But they are sounding better.
E major 7th.
E major 7th.
A major 7th.
A major 7th.

Eight _____

I don't usually keep secrets from my mother. Because I don't have to.

At least I *haven't* had to. Because there hasn't been anything much to not tell her.

Except about wearing makeup. Which I didn't tell her because I only did it once. As an experiment.

Today I'm doing it again.

Today is Friday.

Michaelday.

Michaelday III.

The first time, at the mall.

The second time at Eddie Nova's Guitar Institute.

And today.

Michaelday III.

I am in my room. Which right now is a mess.

The door is closed and I am "putting on my face."

There is a thing that happens to you when you put on makeup. It's not that you change. It's more that that. As the makeup goes on, you feel yourself gathering the courage to be whoever it is you are.

Makeup doesn't make you older as much as it makes you bolder.

As I apply the robin's-egg-blue eye liner to my twitching eyelid—hold still!—I am working up the nerve to walk into that room.

Michael's room.

But, of course, the first thing I have to do is get out of the house without my mother seeing me in my makeup.

Maybe she wouldn't throw a full-out scene at me. (I don't think she would.) But she'd certainly want to know what it—my makeup—was all about.

Which would take time.

Which I haven't very much of.

I have come home from school. To change into the clothes I was wearing the first time.

Fortunately, I was dressed fairly foxy.

I don't always dress foxy.

I frequently dress schlumpy.

At the moment, I am rather foxy.

I am wearing this semi-see-through cream-colored top which is actually like a natural cotton sweater with an open weave.

The top belts at my hips and falls over the top of my pants.

Which are tight.

And high leather boots.

Out.

Over my tight pants.

I am also wearing my face.

A harmless secret I mean to keep from my mother.

She is in her room, which is just across the hallway from my room. She is talking on the phone.

I've got about twenty-seven minutes to get a bus, go to Hackensack, walk over to Fulton Street, climb the stairs, pay Eddie.

I lift my guitar case off the bed.

As quietly as I can, I turn the doorknob and open the door.

Across the way, my mother is still on the phone. She hasn't heard the door. She isn't looking my way.

I will close the door behind me and head for the stairs.

It *clicks*.

Loudly.

"Jessie?" Mom says, interrupting her phone call.

"Bye, Mom," I say. And I lift my guitar case high in the air, so it covers my face. And, hiding behind my guitar case, I head for the stairs.

"Have a good guitar lesson," she calls.

"You, too," I tell her.

And I hit the top of the stairs and down I go, two steps at a time.

And I'm out the front door and racing for the bus stop.

Here I come, Hackensack.

Here I come, Michael.

Ready or not.

Here I come.

Nine

"Hi, Michael," I say.

"Hiya," he answers.

That's *it!*

"Hiya."

He doesn't look up from his guitar.

He doesn't interrupt his noodling.

Just "Hiya."

Nothing else.

I am crushed.

I mean, I'd hoped this was going to be a big reunion between the Handsome Young Rock Star and the Eye-Catching Mystery Girl from the shopping mall. But that is not what this is going to be.

This is going to be a guitar lesson.

Swell.

I unpack my guitar and take a chair, facing Michael.

At last he gives up concentrating on his precious noodling. He actually looks up from his guitar and looks at me.

His eyes do not go wide with recognition.

Or admiration.

They crinkle, in fact, as Michael floats his warm smile over to me.

He is very good-looking.

And quite nice, I think.

Aside from being talented.

I'm glad I practiced.

I play for Michael.

E major 7th.

E major 7th.

A major 7th.

A major 7th.

Not bad, either.

After a while, Michael joins in, strumming a lazy galloping thing that slips underneath my careful picking and lifts it—ever so slightly—off the ground and into the general area of what you could call *music*.

With Michael's help, I am playing *music!*

It feels terrific!

I forget how shattered I feel that Michael didn't recognize his Long-Lost Love, the Famous Mystery Girl from the shopping mall.

I forget about all that stuff and just sort of mellow out on the music, the simple but nice music that Michael and I are making together.

I can't tell you how long this goes on. But not long enough for me. It could never be long enough.

But after a while—a minute or a month—Michael changes the game.

He gives up his galloping strum and falls in with me, picking away at the same two chords I'm picking away at, playing along with me in what they call unison.

This sounds nice, but not as nice as it sounded the other way.

It turns out that this is the launching pad for the teaching part of the lesson.

There is not too much you can play if you only know two chords. Even if you know them fairly well.

So Michael plays along with me, playing just the two chords for a while, and then he plays this *third* chord.

"New chord," he says, and he shows me how he's got his fingers on the guitar strings.

Well, I try to get my fingers to do the same thing on my guitar, but my little finger has a mind of its own and just refuses to do what it's supposed to.

"No," says Michael. "Here."

And he reaches over and lifts my little finger and gentles it into place.

Now, ordinarily, you'd think Michael's touching me like that would freak me out. But the thing is, I realize that some small amount of touching is necessary, if you're going to teach someone how to play the guitar. It's the same for a boy as it is for a girl. Your teacher will sometimes touch you.

He'll move your finger from the wrong string to the right string. Or he'll jiggle the wrist of your strumming hand and try to get you to loosen up your strumming.

The point is, there's nothing sexy in this kind of touching.

I realize that.

But it freaks me out, anyway.

Michael's touching me freaks me out!!

I mean, when he takes my little finger between his thumb and his index finger!

It's like a kiss!

I swear.

Imagine what an *actual* kiss would be like!

No.

Don't imagine that.

Steady.

F# major 7th.

F# major 7th.

That's the name of the new chord. It fits together with the first two chords and, together—the way Michael played them—the three chords sound something like the beginning of a song.

"Put 'em all together, now," Michael tells me. I guess he's satisfied that I can play the new chord.

I actually play the three chords, one after another, without too much fumbling.

Michael's pleased.

So am I.

I keep playing the three chords and Michael does his lazy galloping strum under them and now it *really* sounds like the beginning of a song.

And every time I look up from my guitar, Michael's looking at me. And smiling. Encouraging me, you know?

I could hang on his look forever. And I'd like to. But if I don't keep my eyes on my guitar, the music will fall to pieces, and if that happens, I know the whole mood we've got going will shatter and fall to the floor with a thud.

This is the best time I've ever had in my life!

It lasts quite a while, too.

Until Michael decides it's time to teach me another chord.

"Now, we need a finish," he says. He stops playing.

"If you don't put a finish on it," he says, "it just hangs in your head and clutters up your closets."

I feel the same way about cluttered closets. Except I never thought about the ones in my head. I suppose they must be a mess.

Michael lifts his guitar and he's thinking.

He picks out the three chords we've been playing. They do sound kind of unfinished. Like I said, they sound like the *beginning* of a song.

And you know how a song that begins but doesn't end can haunt you? Well, these three chords are like that.

So Michael's looking for a fourth chord. A chord that will end the song.

And unclutter his closets.

He's got one.

He plays it.

"That's nice," I tell him. It really is. It's satisfying.

"Fourth fret," he says, showing me how to hold my fingers to play the chord.

It's not too hard.

Not by itself.

But then Michael says, "Okay, put a finish on it." And he gets up and walks over to the other side of the room, expecting me to just dash off all four chords, one right after another, without a hitch.

"Okay," I say. And I stand up and put my foot up on the chair and get a good grip of my guitar.

I take a deep breath and I plunge into it.

E major 7th.

E major 7th.

A major 7th.

Not a hitch.

A major 7th.

F# major 7th.

I'm rolling right along.

F# major 7th.

And I can't remember the last chord. The finish!

It's vanished!

So—I give the guitar a whack.

Whack!

And I sing.

"Good evening, friends!"

At the top of my lungs.

And then I take a bow from the waist.

And Michael laughs.

"Not bad," he says, walking back over to me. "Not half bad."

"It's nothin'," I say, trying to toss it off.

"If you say so," says Michael, agreeing with me when he's not supposed to.

But he's just teasing.

"Actually," he says, "it was pretty good."

He lifts the guitar out of my hands and starts playing it, like he does.

"You've been practicing," he says, strumming and kind of ambling around the room.

"Some," I tell him, hoping he hasn't noticed the blisters.

"Well," he says, "you're off to a fast start."

Which is good news to me.

"Yeah?" I say.

"Yeah," he says. "There's no telling how far you might go."

"How far?" I ask him.

I'm not sure if he's talking about my guitar playing or something else!

"You might be real good," he says.

I mean, he could be talking about anything!

"There's no telling," he says.

There's no telling!

"Anyway," he says, still strumming and ambling, and not looking at the little girl who is, slowly but surely, going to pieces, right there, in the middle of a classroom at the Eddie Nova Guitar Institute in downtown Hackensack, New Jersey, U.S.A., where sex education is a joke.

Steady.

"Anyway," he says, "it sure is nice working with somebody who really cares."

He knows!

"Somebody who cares enough to throw herself into it, body and soul," he says.

And he's stopped strumming.

And he's stopped ambling.

And he's standing right in front of me!

Thisclose!

"What time is it?"

I blurt it out.

Which kind of throws him.

And tickles him, too.

He reaches into the pocket of his jeans. They're so tight, you wouldn't think he could even get his hand in there. But he can. And when it comes back out, it's got a watch in it.

A pocket watch. Like a railroad conductor's. Very old. It's silver and it's got a silver cover over its face.

Michael opens the cover with an easy flick of his thumbnail and looks inside.

"Six-fourteen," he says.

"I gotta go," I tell him.

And I grab my guitar and head for my guitar case, over by the door.

"Where you headed?"

"Home," I tell him.

"What happens if you're late? You turn into a pumpkin?"

Well, I don't want Michael thinking I've got some kind of curfew or something. Like some junior high school girl might have. That'd ruin everything.

Not that there's anything to ruin.

"My father's a diabetic," I tell him.

It's not true, strictly speaking.

In fact, it isn't true at all.

"And if he doesn't get his dinner on time," I continue. (Now that I've started, what else can I do but continue?)

"He goes into shock," I conclude.

"Oh," says Michael.

I didn't mean to bring him down.

"Where do you live?" he says.

"Englewood," I tell him.

And I grab up my guitar, which I've finally got packed up in its case.

"Bye," I say.

And I break for the door.

"You want a lift?" he says.

He drives!

"Uh . . ." I answer.

I am standing at the door.

I am looking back over my shoulder at Michael.

And I say, "Uh . . ."

Ten _____

Do you have any idea how far it is from Hackensack to Englewood?

I don't mean miles.

I mean hours.

Hackensack is *several days'* drive from Englewood.

If you're me and Michael is driving you home.

Michael's car is a station wagon with no wood and no plastic pretending to be wood. It's just a plain—very plain—1970-ish station wagon. Dark-green.

And rust.

Around the edges.

Michael has it because he has to haul the instruments and amps—the Skye Band's equipment—around.

I can't think of anything to say.

And Michael doesn't need to say anything.

He's humming to himself. To be exact.

Which should be relaxing for me.

But nothing's relaxing for me.

"I can get a bus from here."

It's another blurt. And I *can't* get a bus from here. But it gets the ball rolling anyway.

"Now, why would you do that?" Michael wants to know.

We are entering the second week of our cross-country drive.

"I like to read the ads," I tell him.

He laughs.

"Look," he says, "it's *my* fault if you're late.

"But," he says, "I was havin' *such* a good time."

"Have you always lived in Englewood?" I ask him.

Blurt!

"No," he says, looking puzzled. It *is* a weird question.

"Oh," I say.

I have nothing more to say.

Another week passes.

Englewood seems no closer.

"We moved up from Atlanta," he says—drawls, now that I think of it, just a little, very nice! "About two years ago. Two years ago this month."

He talks real slow. Like he's not in a hurry and imagines you're not in a hurry, either.

You can hear the sound of the tires on the highway and the wind rushing by in the spaces between his sentences.

"My dad's company gave him a promotion," he says, "to the New York office. With my father's company, you either move up or you move out. So he moved up. And my mother moved out. I guess she missed Atlanta."

He says all this with a smile on his face. And he says it like it's an easy thing to tell. But you can tell it isn't all that easy.

"I guess you miss Atlanta, too," I tell him.

"Huh?" he says. He was daydreaming, out there, down the road.

Probably in Atlanta.

With his mom.

"Yeah," he says, playing back the tape of our conversation, finding his place.

"Yeah, I guess."

He looks surprised. Maybe because he told me—somebody he hardly knows—more than he meant to tell me. You get the feeling he doesn't talk about himself all that much.

"You always lived in Englewood?" he asks.

And he's teasing me.

"So far," I tell him.

And we both laugh together.

We are getting closer to Englewood. With a tailwind, we could make it before the end of the month.

"Twining Court's near Beardsley Park, isn't it?"

I am not listening.

I am noticing how dark it is getting.

But one word jumps out at me.

"Park?" I blurt.

He doesn't notice.

"I jog there," he explains.

"Jogging!" I say, not missing a beat. "Great sport! Great sport."

"You jog?"

"Oh," I lie, "sure! Doesn't everybody?"

"In Beardsley Park?" he asks.

"It's so handy," I tell him.

Why am I doing this?

"I jog every Sunday morn—"

"Saturdays!" I blurt.

Which, of course, is why he hasn't bumped into me all those thousands of times I've gone jogging in good old Beardsley Park.

"Oh," he says, disappointed.

"But sometimes on Sundays," I add.

It seems to help.

"I go about nine," he says.

He goes jogging!

On Sunday mornings!

At nine o'clock!

"Twelve," I tell him.

That's when I do my jogging.

I lie around the clock.

Why am I lying?

Listen to the tires.

Listen to the wind.

Listen to Michael, humming.

Michael humming is sexier than Royal Dalton kissing the upturned palm of Jasmine's hand.

"Do you mind if I ask you a question?" says Michael.

"I can't tell until you ask," I answer.

"Fair enough," says Michael, and he looks over at me, looks me right in the eye, and says, "How old are you?"

"Sixteen," I say.

Now, I know why I lied about the jogging. I knew this was coming. I was practicing!

I wait for the lightning to strike.

It is busy elsewhere.

"Sixteen," I say again.

"How come I haven't seen you around school?" he says.

"That's *two* questions," I tell him, buying myself some time.

How come he hasn't seen me around school if I'm from Englewood and sixteen and he's from Englewood and he's seventeen?

"I go to Immaculate, the parochial high school. In Dellwood."

The Church of St. John the Baptist has just made a miraculous appearance at the end of this street. I am an instant convert.

As Michael turns the corner in front of the church, I risk hellfire and damnation.

I cross myself.

"Us Catholic kids," I tell Michael, "we keep pretty much to ourselves, you know?"

Where am I getting this stuff?

"That," says Michael, "is a real shame."

We are turning into my street.

Pulling up to my house.

"This one?"

"Yeah."

"Bye," says Michael.

"Bye," says Jessie.

And Michael pulls away.

And turns on his headlights.

Because it is dark.

Well after sundown.

Jessie runs into her house.

To light the Sabbath candles.

Three weeks late!

Boy, am I gonna get it!

Eleven _____

I almost forget the makeup.

I get halfway to the front door and I flash on it.

I fish the cold cream out of my bag.

"For when you're ready to be thirteen, again."

"Oh, I don't think I'll ever be ready for that!"

I have most of it off by the time I enter the back door.

"Jessie?"

It's my mom, calling from the dining room.

She's mad.

"Yes, Mom?" I answer, swabbing the last of the cold cream off my eyelids.

"You're late!" my mom says, charging in to meet me.

"I know," I say. "I'm sorry."

"Well, come on," she says.

And I drop my guitar case and my bag and follow her into the dining room.

My father is reading the paper. He looks up from it as mom and I come into the room.

"We tried to hold the sunset for you," he says. "But you know how it is." He shrugs.

I thank him for trying.

The thing is, if you're Jewish, you're supposed to light Sabbath candles at sunset on Friday nights.

The fact is, I don't go to Immaculate and I'm not Catholic—I go to J.F.K. Junior High and I'm Jewish. And I lie, if necessary, and it is already the Sabbath and the candles haven't been lit, yet.

Because I usually light them. And they were waiting for me.

So, I light the Sabbath candles.

The family—Mom and Dad and Grandma—all gather around. And I light the candles, one by one. And as I light the candles I say this prayer—in Hebrew.

Blessed art thou,

O Lord,

Our God,

King of the Universe,

Who has sanctified us by thy Commandments

And who has commanded us to kindle the Sabbath lights.

Amen.

And then, when all the candles are lit, we all hug each other in the candlelight.

And then I help my mom serve dinner.

And clear.

My father helps her clean up.

It's a nice way to start the weekend.

Quietly.

With a little respect.

So, I finish lighting the candles and saying the prayer.

And everybody says "Amen."

And I hug my grandma.

And my father.

And my mother.

And I'm forgiven.

Mom puts her arm around my shoulder and walks with me toward the kitchen.

"How was your lesson?" she says.

"Okay," I tell her.

It's the truth. As far as it goes.

Twelve _____

I like to sleep late Sunday mornings.

It is eight-fourteen.

So, it's surprising that I'm up and around so early *this* Sunday morning.

What's also surprising is the way I'm dressed.

Like a jogger.

I'm going jogging.

In Beardsley Park.

I'm going to "bump into" Michael.

I know.

It's corny.

That's why I decided against it.

Last night.

Just before I fell asleep.

It wasn't an easy decision.

I've thought about it since Friday, when Michael said he jogged in Beardsley Park every Sunday morning.

"I go about nine."

"Twelve."

"Do you mind if I ask you a question?"

The thing is, I like Michael.

So, I thought I'd like to see Michael.

But the more I see Michael, the more I like him.

And if I liked Michael any more than I already do—
It would be impossible!

Michael is seventeen, I've decided.

I am thirteen. My parents decided that fourteen years ago.

Thirteen-year-old girls are too young for seventeen-year-old boys. And vice versa. The world decided that.

Of course, once upon a time the world also decided it was flat.

But that's not the point.

The whole world would be against us—my parents (I'm pretty sure), Caroline, Michael's friends, his parents.

They'd all be against us!

And they'd make it impossible.

Or we would.

I mean, Michael could just go on thinking I'm sixteen, like I told him.

And we could go to places where nobody'd see us or nobody'd recognize us.

And we could be left alone.

To—

That's the thing.

Left alone to what?

I mean, when it comes right down to it—

If it should come right down to it—

If I was left alone with Michael—

If Michael was left alone with me—

I don't think I could handle it!

Some girls my age can.

And some do.

But I don't think *I* could.

I can't even think about it!

Like—

I'm in this cabin.

Up in the mountains.

By a lake.

It's a summer resort, but this is winter and there's no one around for miles and miles.

You can hear the sound of the wind in the pines.

And the crackle of the fire.

I am curled in front of the fire.

Wearing just my robe.

Looking into the fire.

Sipping sassafras tea from an earthen mug.

Michael's at the door.

It is Christmas, and he's gone out to find us a tree.

He opens the door and all you can see is the tree— full and plump and dusted with fresh-fallen snow—and

Michael's hand, reaching in from the side, holding the tree up, straight and tall.

"Ta-dah!" he trumpets.

"Oh, Michael," I say.

And I put down my tea.

And gathering my robe about me, I go to greet him.

"It's fabulous!" I tell him.

"So are you," says Michael, moving into the doorway, entering the cabin, smiling, covered with snow.

"You're all wet," I tell him.

He laughs and shakes his head and the snow falls from his hair, down over his shoulders and down the front of his jacket.

I reach up and unzip his jacket.

Beneath his jacket, his chest is bare.

And flecked with melting snowflakes.

Running in tiny, glistening streams.

Running down his chest.

My robe is belted at the waist.

Michael smiles.

Reaches out.

Unfastens my belt.

I feel my robe opening—

Falling away—

I—

Whoa!

That's it!

As far as I go!

I mean it!

I mean, it makes me crazy to even think of going any further!

So, how could I handle it in real life?

I couldn't!

So, even if the whole world wasn't against us—

Even if they left us alone—

It would be impossible!

I'd make it impossible.

Probably.

So, what's the point of going jogging in the park and bumping into Michael?

What's the point of seeing Michael more and liking Michael more?

69

When I know it would be impossible?

No point.

That's what I decided.

Last night.

Just before I went to sleep.

But when I woke up early this morning, I put on my cut-offs and my sneakers.

And I put on a little makeup.

I'm going jogging.

In Beardsley Park.

With Michael.

Ta-dah!

Thirteen _____

Beardsley Park is this especially pretty park that is conveniently located in my neighborhood in Englewood.

I almost never go there.

I am not the athletic type.

But Beardsley Park is very pretty.

The trees come right down to the edge of the lake—like wild animals, coming to drink at a jungle water hole. And there's this jogging path that winds under the trees, all around the edge of the lake. So you can run through the woods in the shade of the trees and catch glimpses of this nice cool lake.

This combination seems to appeal to joggers. I imagine that jogging around the reservoir is like playing a suburban version of Indian.

Anyway, about the only place the woods don't come all the way down to the edge of the lake is this clearing I'm in. There's a statue here. A statue of Mercury.

Mercury and I are keeping a lookout, combing the trees along the edge of the reservoir, looking for Michael.

The idea is, I'll spot Michael, coming around the reservoir, and I'll run up onto the jogging path and start jogging away until he catches up with me.

I am hoping that by the time Michael catches up with me, he will have had about enough of jogging, so I won't have to actually jog all that much.

So I am standing in this clearing in the bright spring sunlight, checking out this totally naked statue and throwing glances into the trees around the reservoir, looking for signs of approaching Michaelness.

Mercury used to be a Greek god, but he fell on hard

times and went to work delivering telegrams for Western Union. This explains how well developed his legs are. And his thighs. And—

There's somebody coming!

An older man.

Somebody whose doctor told him jogging would be good for him. It sure doesn't look like it's fun. Chug, chug, chug.

So, Mercury, what's happening?

Is it true what they say about you Greek gods? That you're all ladies' men and not above changing into regular male human beings just for the sake of having a good time with an unsuspecting Earth lady?

I bet it is.

You've got that look about you.

I look about me.

Somebody else is coming along the jogging path.

Several somebodies.

None of them Michael.

Maybe he decided not to jog today.

Maybe he decided to jog at twelve, when I told him I'd be jogging. Maybe he's planning on bumping into me.

Nah.

What would happen if Mercury turned into a regular male human being right now? Would he be so handsome and godly (and naked) that I couldn't resist him?

Would he whisper sweet nothings and steer me into the woods and get me drunk on elderberry wine and—

Michael's coming!

Sorry, Mercury! I hate to leave you like this, but you know how it is with us Earth ladies!

I turn my back on Mercury and dash onto the jogging path.

I am on the path and chugging along at a pretty good clip.

Before Michael catches up with me I am panting like a steam locomotive.

Black spots are dancing before my eyes.

My ankles are wobbly.

This is *before* Michael catches up to me.

"Hey!" he says, falling in next to me.

"Michael!" I gasp, trying to cover the struggle on my face with a look of astonishment.

"You got an early start," he says.

"Yeah," I answer. "Out since eight."

"Great day, huh?"

"Yeah."

"Nice park, too," he says. He says more. But that's all *I* hear.

I have fallen from exhaustion. I am lying down.

On the jogging path.

The jig is up.

The jog is over.

I do not jog.

I am not the athletic type.

I am not the sixteen type, either.

I am a fraud.

A phony.

Leave me alone.

Please.

I want to die.

I have killed myself.

Jogging.

"Hey, you all right?"

Through the darkness, I recognize his voice.

I open my eyes.

Michael is standing over me. Looking down at me, lying across the jogging path, at his feet.

He looks concerned. And scared. Scared for *me*.

"Twisted ankle," I tell him. And I close my eyes.

Because I can't face him.

And I want to die.

"Can you stand?" he says. Through the darkness. But close!

Thisclose!

I open my eyes.

Michael's face is thisclose to mine.

His eyes thisclose to my eyes.

His mouth thisclose to my mouth.

I am speechless.

I have died.

"Come on," he says. And he takes my two hands in his. "I'll give you a hand."

And he pulls me up onto my feet.

My *foot*.

Twisted ankle.

I lift my left foot off the ground. Like it hurts.

I cringe a little. From the pain.

He puts his arm around my waist and pulls me close to him, so I can lean on him while I walk.

"Best thing for it," he says, "is to keep jogging on it."

I suppose bullets are also good for bullet wounds.

"Yeah," I say.

"See you," I say.

And I disentangle myself from him.

And I head off toward the park entrance and home.

I was right last night.

This is totally impossible.

"Hey," he says. And he's right beside me again. He jogged up beside me. "Don't you want a hand?"

He's making this very difficult.

Considering that I'm dead, especially.

"No," I tell him. "I'm okay. And besides," I say, nodding back toward the jogging path, "I wouldn't want to spoil your fun."

And I turn and walk away again.

"Walking's good for it, too," he says.

He's done it again. Jogged up to me.

"Uh-huh," I tell him.

"But if you'd like a ride," he says.

Michael!

I'm trying to do you a favor, here!

I'm thirteen!

Get it?

"No," I say, "it's not that far. And besides, walking's supposed to be good for it."

"And cold water," he reminds me. Tagging right along.

We walk, together—he walks, I limp—to the park entrance. To do this, we have to walk through the park.

This morning I thought the park was beautiful.

Well, when you walk through the park with Michael walking beside you, it is *extremely* beautiful! You want to eat it up. The park. You want to eat it up and swallow

74

it. That's how beautiful it is, walking—limping—through Beardsley Park with Michael by your side.

Michael's car is parked in the parking lot near the entrance to the park. It's beautiful, too.

And I don't think I'm dead, anymore.

I think I'm very alive.

"You want to come to rehearsal tomorrow? After school?" he says.

To be or not to be?

That was the question Lance Cantrell's offer now posed for the lovely Melinda Bliss . . .

"It's not like a concert or anything," he says.

It would be so easy to refuse him.

To refuse herself.

So easy.

"The fact is, it can get pretty boring. Not for us, but— you know—for people. Not when we're playing . . ."

And yet, she knew.

With all her heart and soul, she knew.

". . . but sometimes at rehearsals. So what do you think?" he says.

"Rehearsal?" I say, coming out of it. "Sure."

"Great," he says.

He'll pick me up.

After school.

At Immaculate.

"Three-thirty?" he asks.

"Uhh . . ." I calculate. "Yyyeah."

"Bring your guitar, okay?"

"Okay," I say.

"Three-thirty," he says.

"Immaculate," I say.

"In Dellwood," he says.

"Yeah," I say.

"Bye, Jessie."

"Goodbye, Michael."

I turn and jog away.

"Hey," Michael calls after me.

"It's better, my ankle," I assure him.

I come from a long line of fast healers. And liars.

"Good," says Michael.

"Bye," I answer.

And I'm off and running. But I can't resist taking one last look back.

Michael is standing by his car door, shaking his head, smiling. I can tell by the way he looks that he thinks I'm a little weird. I can also tell that he likes me.

But why my guitar?

Fourteen ─────────────────────────────

JFK gets out at three.

Half an hour before Immaculate.

Which is about twenty-five minutes away, by bus.

So, I can just about make it.

Except JFK doesn't *actually* get out at three, because Mr. Silvestre—our principal—has this microphone in his office and these loudspeakers on every classroom wall and he's a ham.

At three—when we should be getting out—Mr. Silvestre gets on the loudspeaker and starts hamming it up. He does it every day.

Today, it's about hanging around the school grounds after school, which is forbidden unless you're engaged in "healthy recreational activities."

It seems that hanging around the school grounds after school without a basketball in your hands or something makes people nervous. Just which people isn't too clear. But whoever they are, they're a lot more important than we are. Especially if all we're doing is hanging around the school grounds after school without a basketball in our hands or something.

Hanging around the school grounds after school is not my problem.

Getting to Immaculate before three-thirty is my problem.

It is now three-oh-four.

And Mr. Silvestre isn't finished.

"And *do* be careful crossing the streets on your *ways* home," he says. "Do not loiter. Do not litter. And remember—Tuesday is Class Day and we're expecting all of you to show all of us a little class."

Har-har.

"This is Mr. Silvestre, your principal, speaking."

And speaking and speaking!

"Bell," he says.

That's how he always finishes. He tells himself to ring the bell and then he rings it.

Ring!

And everybody bolts for the door.

Me and Caroline lead the pack.

Side by side, walking as fast as we can—you're not permitted to run, even if there's a fire—Caroline and I race down the corridor, heading for the front door.

"Are you nervous?" Caroline asks me.

"Do I look nervous?" I ask her, flashing her my famous cover-girl smile.

"Yeah," she says.

I have to admit it. I *am* nervous. I've never been to a rehearsal before and I imagine there'll be a lot of Michael's friends there. Older kids.

"Yeah."

"Me, too," says Caroline.

"Yeah?" I say.

"I'm going to the dentist," she breathes.

"Oh," I say.

"Dr. Donnie!" she reminds me.

"The hip-kisser?"

"Yeah," she sighs. "It's our quarterly checkup."

"Yours and his?"

"Yeah," she swoons.

"Caroline?" I ask her. "Do you think older men are worth it?"

"Oh, yeah," she gushes.

"Me, too," I admit.

We hit the front door, and I say goodbye and take off, running for the bus stop.

Lucky for me, there's a bus just pulling into the bus stop, and running as fast as I can and toting my guitar case like a bag of laundry, I just make it.

I pick a seat, put my guitar case across my lap—making a kind of table out of it—and get out my makeup.

78

I have decided that I will always wear makeup around Michael.

Maybe it's just for good luck. The second lesson did go better than the first lesson. I mean, Michael drove me home! And then, jogging in the park. When he invited me to the rehearsal.

Maybe it doesn't actually make me *look* older.

Maybe it just makes me *feel* older.

Or makes other people feel I'm older.

There will probably be a lot of other people at the rehearsal. Michael's friends. I'd like them to feel I'm older.

As well as Michael.

And me, of course.

I'd like all of us to feel I'm older.

We get to Immaculate at three-twenty-eight. There's a big clock on this spire in the middle of Immaculate, and that's what it says, as the bus is pulling up.

And I am late.

Because Michael's already arrived and he's sitting in his car, right in front of the school, waiting for me to pop out the front door, any second.

I pop out the door of the *bus.*

Without Michael seeing me.

Then run along the hedges that stretch from the curb near the bus stop all the way to the back of the school.

These hedges are long, but they are not tall. I run stooped over.

And carrying my guitar case.

Then scoot around the back of the school.

Pop in the back door.

I am in the corridor of Immaculate and the bell is ringing and all these girls—it's all girls at Immaculate— are pouring out of the rooms.

Wearing uniforms.

I am not wearing a uniform.

They are wearing uniforms.

Michael will notice.

They will notice.

They do.

"Hiya," I say.

"How you doin'?"

79

"Nice day, huh?"

I walk along with them, among them, all the way out the front door and down the long, long sidewalk that runs right down to the front door of Michael's car, parked at the curb.

Michael!

I wave.

He waves.

He didn't see me get off the bus.

"See you tomorrow," I call to this knot of girls, standing near the car in their uniforms, kind of half-checking Michael out.

He is gorgeous!

I wave to them.

And they're actually waving back, as I climb into Michael's car.

"Take care," one of them says.

"Sorry I'm late," I tell Michael. "I had to change."

I've done it.

I've made it.

I can handle it.

"That's okay," says Michael. "But now you got me wondering what you look like in your uniform."

He says this with this grin on his face—a grin that could melt butter.

"Like them," I tell him, and I nod to the knot of girls who are still standing around in their uniforms.

"Nah," he says, still grinning, "I bet you look just like you."

"Michael!" I say. I say it like, "Cut it out, okay?"

"It's okay with me," he says. "I kind of like the way you look."

I am melted butter.

"Michael! Rehearsal!"

I am starting to sizzle!

He backs off, thank God. He drifts his attention from me over to the steering wheel.

"And step on it!" I tell him.

So cool.

"Say it again," he says.

He doesn't start the car.

"Step on it?" I ask him.

"Nope."

"Rehearsal?"

"Uh-uh."

I know what he wants me to say.

He wants me to say his name.

While he's looking into my eyes!

Deep breath.

"Michael."

My voice doesn't quaver.

My face doesn't twitch.

My head doesn't bobble around at the end of my neck.

It just feels that way.

But Michael holds his eyes on mine and, real warm and even, he says, "It sounds good, the way you say it, Jessie."

I pray that he won't ask me to say it again.

If I tried—I know it!—I'd quaver.

And twitch.

And bobble.

My prayer is answered.

Michael starts the car.

Good.

Because Michael, coming right at you like that— Michael is too much!

Fifteen ─────────────────────

Michael's band rehearses in this empty factory in Paterson.

They rent it from somebody's uncle for not much money, since otherwise it's just standing there, empty.

It's a pretty long ride to the factory, but not as long as it was getting started.

I mean, I am nervous about meeting Michael's friends, but not half as nervous as I was just being with Michael at Immaculate.

Also, Michael isn't being super-sexy anymore. Not super-super-sexy like he was.

He's just driving. And we're listening to the radio. And talking, over the music.

Like two regular people.

Except after a while, Michael wants to know more about my family.

"They mostly go to church," I tell Michael, "and save their money. For the trip to Rome. To see the Pope. It's their dream."

I'm getting good at this. But there's no sense pressing my luck.

"What about your family?"

"My family?" he says.

"Unless you'd rather not—"

"No, it's okay," he says.

But I can see it's not.

They're not very happily divorced.

Michael's mother goes to college in Atlanta. She always wanted to be a painter.

Except she never told anybody about it until she decided not to move to Englewood with Michael and his father. That's when it came out about her wanting to be a painter and go to college and have Michael's father pay for everything.

Which he does. Michael's father. He pays for Michael's mother, going to college and everything else. That's the way they worked it out.

Michael's father also pays for himself and for Michael, although Michael pretty much pays his own way.

Anyway, Michael's father has to work a lot and doesn't get to spend much time with Michael. Except on weekends.

"That's when I see him mostly," Michael tells me. "When I see him, I try to cheer him up, as best I can. But the thing is, he doesn't even know he's sad. And that makes it kind of hard, you know? I keep trying, though. Alex sure could use a winning hand."

"Maybe you're it," I tell him. He could be.

"Yeah," says Michael, not quite agreeing with me, "maybe."

But you can see he doesn't think so. You can see he doesn't think anything's going to make it all right for his father. Except maybe his father. If he wants to. Which, I guess, he doesn't.

It's pretty depressing.

Even if Michael pretends it's not.

I'm sorry I brought it up.

But it's nice that Michael told me. That he confided in me. I can tell that he doesn't do that a lot and it makes me feel good that he'd do it with me. As if we were already old friends.

That's what it feels like.

Comfortable.

A little.

Driving to rehearsal with Michael.

It isn't hard at all, to forget about all the tension before.

"Say it again."

"Step on it?"

It isn't too hard to forget that I'm on my way to being inspected by Michael's friends for telltale signs of youth.

Like small breasts.

84

And amateur makeup.

And being tonguetied.

"Nice to meet you."

"Uh . . ."

I expect there will be lots of high school "groupies" around Michael and the Skye Band. And I expect that their supersensitive child detectors will start beeping before we even get close to the factory.

But I'm not thinking about that at the moment. I'm in a cushiony steel cocoon. With Michael. And music. And trees rushing by. And I'm thinking about my future.

Michael asked me.

"Well . . . I hope I'll grow up to be . . ."

How should I say it?

"Growing up, all the time," I tell him.

It's not exactly what I mean.

"You know what I mean?" I ask Michael.

"Not exactly," he admits.

"I mean . . . I don't want to be *anything*. Any one thing. I mean, there's no *one* thing I want to be . . . except alive. And happy. And . . ."

I have to take a deep breath to get this one out.

"And good," I say.

"Sounds real ambitious," says Michael.

At first I can't tell if he means it, but when I look at his face, I know he does.

"What about wanting to be a rock star?" I ask him.

It's a question Michael's thought about before. He'd have had to. He so obviously is a rock star, already.

"No," he says, "I've got my hands full, just trying to be a good musician. That's not the same thing. For one thing, it's harder. And it takes longer. Being a rock star, that's a whole different thing."

"You could be as big as Peter Frampton!" I tell him.

"Yeah," he says, "or Paul Williams."

I laugh.

It's one thing to be handsome and talented and nice. Having a sense of humor besides is definitely unfair.

"Anyway," he says, "how would *you* know?"

He's playing with me.

"You can tell," I tell him.

Playing with *him*.

"Can you?" he says.

"Well," I say, reconsidering, "now, I'm not so sure."

"Damn!" he says, and he bangs the palm of his hand against the steering wheel.

Michael's only playing, of course. Like I've been.

Still, I don't want to leave it this way.

"I'm sure," I tell him.

It's real hard to say. Like saying "Michael" was, back at Immaculate. Because it's saying what you know he wants to hear. Which is kind of like saying "I like you."

And—although it must be pretty obvious how much I like Michael—it would still be very hard to say.

"I like you, Michael."

Because it's so serious, I guess. I guess that's what makes it scary.

"There'll be a few people there," says Michael.

He's talking about rehearsal.

We're approaching the factory!

I was so relaxed.

But now—!

"Friends," he says, "former friends, future friends—of mine and the other guys'."

They will examine me!

They will dissect me!

"They're good people," says Michael, pulling up to the factory. "You'll fit right in."

Like a boat at an auto show.

We drive *into* the factory, up this ramp to the second floor, which is this huge garage with sunlit windows in all the walls and skylights all over the ceiling.

As we drive in, there's this cheer for Michael—for his car, actually, because the cheer starts as soon as the hood of Michael's car appears at the top of the ramp, long before anyone could actually see his face.

Which is smiling.

Michael's a little embarrassed at the commotion, but he's a little proud of it, too.

There's maybe seventy-five or a hundred kids applauding and cheering, as Michael (and me) pull into the garage.

They've got their cars parked in a circle, and they're sitting up on top of them—on their roofs and hoods and fenders. They keep on cheering and applauding, until Michael pulls up into the circle of cars.

The Skye Band—there's five of them, besides Michael —is in the center of the circle of cars right under a sky-light, pouring sunshine straight down on them. They've got their amps and horns and stuff all set up. They're tuning up, as Michael climbs out of the car.

Michael deposits me and my guitar case on the hood of his car.

"Now, remember," he says, "I warned you. It's just a rehearsal."

I wish I'd rehearsed feeling like I'm sixteen a little bit more.

"Don't worry about me," I tell Michael.

He turns and moves off to join the band in the center of the circle, under the skylight.

Which leaves me alone.

With all these people.

Staring at me.

Looking me over.

Checking me out.

Especially the girls.

A couple of them smile at me.

I smile back. Kind of a plaster smile. But it passes for the real thing from a distance.

Some nod.

I nod. Like a mechanical toy. But it passes.

Most just look and whisper to each other and giggle.

They're the ones who know I'm not sixteen.

The ones who see through me.

The ones with the most sensitive child-detectors.

I know it's just a matter of time before someone blows the whistle on me.

I expect the Enforcement Section of the Uniformed Babysitters Bureau to rush in and grab me and haul me away any second now.

But Michael saves me.

"One! Two! Three! Four!"

Michael shouts the cadence to the band and—bam!— they're off and rocking.

And nobody's the least bit interested in me anymore.

I take a deep breath.

I think it's the first time I've breathed since we got here.

It's not bad.

Breathing.

Not bad moving to the music, either.

Sitting up here on the fender, bopping along, dancing with the car's shock absorbers.

Michael and the band are so good!

I mean, except for me, everybody's up on their feet and dancing and clapping their hands.

That's the kind of music it is.

And the kind of rock star Michael is.

His singing—

His playing—

His dancing—

Michael just knocks everybody out!

I forget all about the crowd—the starers and whisperers and gigglers.

I forget all about the people from the Babysitters Bureau.

I forget about everything.

But Michael.

For the longest time, everything else just goes away, and Michael just fills me up and floods me over. There isn't even enough of me left over to hope it never stops, to hope it goes on forever.

But then, as fast as it started—where did the time go? —it stops.

With a roar.

From the band.

And then from the crowd.

"Anybody thirsty?" Michael shouts, asking the band —all of them smiling, happy, and drenched with sweat.

"You know it!"

"Yeah!"

"All right!"

"Water bo-o-o-y!"

Michael and the band come piling out of the center of the circle and into the crowd.

People keep clapping and shouting as they pass, reaching out to shake their hands—a girl throws her arms around the drummer and kisses him—reaching out to just touch them—especially Michael.

Everybody follows Michael and the band to his car!

Where I'm sitting!

Aging as fast as I can!

"How ya' doin'?" says Michael, approaching and—whew!—passing. On his way to the back of the car.

"Fabulous!" I tell him.

Michael smiles.

"Right back," he says. And he leads everybody around to the back of the wagon. And opens up the tailgate.

Michael's got a big cooler in the back of the wagon and it's filled with ice-cold beer. He reaches into the cooler and grabs out cans of beer and tosses them to the people in the band.

Michael takes one, too. He takes it and pops it open and heads back around to the front of the car.

"Beer?" says Michael, sliding up onto the fender across the hood from me. Offering me a taste of his beer.

"No, thank you."

"Not bad, huh?" he says.

"Not half bad," I tell him.

He laughs at that. His easy laugh. And drinks some of his beer.

Some people wander by.

"Sounded good," one of them says.

"Thanks," says Michael. "It's comin'."

"Yeah," says the girl.

"Hi," she says to me.

"Hi," I say.

"Real good," says the guy, moving off.

"It's comin'," says Michael.

"Yeah," says the girl.

"Bye," she says to me.

"Bye."

She didn't look at me funny at all. Not like I had two heads or anything. Like you'd look at a thirteen-year-old girl who was out with Michael, for example.

She was just friendly. And curious, I guess. But nice enough.

So maybe it'll be okay.

"Grab your guitar," says Michael.

Bang! Instant infant.

"Oh, no!"

"Come on."

"I couldn't, Michael!"

"Sure you could," he says.

And he takes my hand!

And he slides down off his fender and pulls me down off my fender and onto my feet.

I reach out and grab my guitar case, at the last minute. But I'm not going anywhere.

"Michael!"

"This is Jessie, everybody!"

We are moving toward the center of the circle. Everybody's looking at us. At me.

I'm smiling. A frozen smile. A smile on a stick.

"Jessie's gonna sit in with us," Michael announces.

Sit in with them?

I play four chords.

"I hope you know what you're doing," I tell Michael.

"Sure." Michael smiles. "All the time!"

And he crosses his eyes and lolls his tongue out the corner of his mouth, just to prove his point.

Really!

And I'm in the center of the circle. With the amps and horns and stuff. With Michael and the Skye Band. With these cars and kids all around. And my guitar case.

"Jessie's a student of mine," says Michael to the band. Like an introduction.

"I'll bet!" one of them says. And he laughs. And so does Michael. And a few other people.

I am busy, taking my guitar out of its case. Not paying attention.

"She's just a beginner," says Michael.

"All right!" says the drummer. And he bashes his cymbal.

They laugh again.

And I'm ready.

As ready as I'll ever be.

"Show 'em, Jess," he says.

I only know the four chords. The ones Michael taught me.

So, I play them.

Not so well.

But right.

"Loosen up," Michael says.

Deep breath.

I loosen up.

It sounds better.

Michael joins in with me.

Strumming that lazy galloping thing.

It sounds okay.

The drummer joins in, too.

Click-click-*click!*

Nice.

Then the organ—high and keening like the song of a locust on a hot summer day.

Eeeeeeeeee!

Now, the bass comes loping in.

Bum-ba-*bum*-ba-*bum!*

So, pretty.

The second guitar, now—running along, frisky, nipping at the heels of Michael's lazy galloping strum.

Chig-a-*dig!* Chig-a-*dig!* Chig-a-*dig!*

And all of a sudden, it's a song!

A song they've built around me and my four chords—the four chords Michael taught me.

Me and my four chords are the star of this song.

And more than that—

This song has words!

Words that Michael's written!

Words he sings to me!

And I'm pretty sure from the look on Michael's face that Michael has written and is singing these words for *me!*

Michael's written me a song!

I can't believe it!

> *And I don't know I knew it,*
> *But I knew it, somehow.*
> *You're the answer to the question*
> *no one answered till now . . .*

91

And I don't know what you see,
What you see in me,
But, girl, it's nothing to
What I see in you . . .

Stars that glisten,
Lips for kissin'.
Honey, listen, it's true—
No one ever
Loved you better.
Love you, honey,
I love you.

He sings like he means every word.
I am floating.
Floating in the music.
In the sound of Michael's voice.
In Michael's eyes.

No one ever
Loved you better.
Love you, honey,
I love you.

The song doesn't end.
One by one, each instrument drops out.
Michael's guitar is the last.
Except for me.
I return from outer space—from the inner space of
Michael's eyes—to discover myself still playing my guitar.
Still playing my four chords—the four chords Michael
taught me.
"Put a finish on it, Jess."
Quickly, I play around to the fourth chord, and when
I get to it, I strum it—slowly and gently—and just let
the notes float up into the air.
You can hear them, just hanging there.
Then, one by one, you can hear them dropping away,
falling away into silence.
But a single voice.
It says, "Michael."
It's my voice.

And this is me.

Jessie.

Throwing my arms around Michael's neck.

Bringing his face down to mine.

Kissing him.

Kissing Michael!

The sound of the drum and the cymbal and the crowd, cheering and applauding, brings me back.

"Jess," he says.

He's smiling.

Surprised.

Happy.

He puts his arm around me now.

He walks me out of the center of the circle.

Rehearsal is over.

On the way home, Michael asks me what I'm doing this Saturday night.

I tell him I don't know.

Rehearsal is over.

Sixteen

I have until Friday to make up my mind.

I have a lesson with Michael on Friday.

I haven't said anything to anybody, yet.

About Michael's asking me out.

Because this is *my* problem.

I know what Caroline would say.

"Older boys aren't like younger boys. They're like men. Only younger!"

Caroline would be particularly rough on older men now, after her visit to Dr. Donnie. It was a great disappointment.

Caroline's teeth were perfect. Dr. Donnie didn't work on her at all. Just the hygienist, who polished Caroline's perfect teeth. So, there was no chance for hip-arm contact. No hip-kissing.

Caroline was crushed.

She went out and bought bags and bags of hard candies. She's had one or two of them in her mouth almost ever since. Caroline's determined to get a cavity. But so far, all she's got is a zit or two.

So there wouldn't be much point in discussing my problem with Caroline.

And as far as my mother and father are concerned, well, why should I upset them and tell them about Michael if there's nothing to tell?

Except that I'm thinking some about going out with this boy—who just happens to be seventeen and incredibly sexy—and I thought it might be nice if they worried about it a lot, until I decided for sure.

Since I've practically decided not to go out with Michael, not to see him—except for guitar lessons—there's really no point in discussing my problem with my parents.

The reason I've practically decided what I've practically decided is kissing Michael.

Kissing Michael surprised me.

I didn't plan on it.

I didn't think about it.

I just found myself doing it!

And Michael doing it back!

It was wonderful!

But I didn't have any control over it.

And that was just kissing!

In public!

What about holding each other?

In private?

I have to be honest.

If I was alone with Michael, in private, I'd probably forget when to say "Stop."

I couldn't trust myself.

And I am afraid.

I mean, if it hadn't been for the drum and the cymbal and the crowd, cheering and yelling, Michael could have done practically anything he wanted to do with me at the factory.

Honestly.

The drum and cymbal and everything were like an alarm clock. And I guess I had plenty to be alarmed about. Because I was gone! Checked out!

Obviously, the only way to make sure I'll remember to say "Stop" is to say it before I start.

Like tomorrow.

At the lesson.

"No, Michael, I can't go out with you . . . I'm sorry . . . In fact, if you want to know . . . it breaks my heart . . . that I can't go out with you . . . tomorrow or ever . . . I'm not . . . I'm not what I seem to be, Michael . . . To begin with . . . I don't go to Immaculate . . ."

It'll be hard.

But it's the right thing to do.

I'm sure of it.

At least I *was!*

Until just now.

I am sitting at dinner with my mother and father and grandma, sipping my soup, and they drop it on me.

It's like a sign.

They've been invited to a wedding.

Saturday night.

This Saturday night!

In New York.

More.

They have been invited, and they are going!

They won't be home until late.

Very late.

Now.

One of the basic rules is "Never look a gift horse in the mouth."

I have never actually seen a gift horse.

But I think one has just trotted into my dining room.

"Saturday seems awful sudden for a wedding," I say. We're on the soup.

"He's a musician, your cousin," says my mother, explaining. "Actually, he's your *second* cousin. Yes. He plays the violin. With an orchestra that doesn't make records."

"Oh," I say.

"They're flighty, musicians," my mother concludes.

I am interested in this cousin—this second cousin of mine. This flighty musician cousin of mine has obviously gotten somebody in trouble. Somebody who, obviously, forgot when to say "Stop."

"Is she pregnant?" I ask.

My father almost chokes on his soup.

"Jessie!" my mother scolds.

My father's trying not to laugh and not doing so well.

"Bob!" says my mother.

"Sorry," he says.

And goes back to his soup.

Grandma's listening and watching.

Grandma doesn't say much. But she doesn't miss much, either.

I think she knows what I'm up to. I mean, weddings, pregnancy, passion. I want to know about these things.

I need to know about these things.

Before Saturday night.

Before tomorrow.

"Saturday is awful sudden, though. Isn't it?" I ask.

"She's not pregnant," says my mother.

"You don't think so?" my father asks.

"Today is Thursday," I chime in.

"I know she's not," my mother tells my father.

"You asked?" he answers.

"Of course not," she says, "Lillian told me. When she called to invite us. This afternoon."

"Too salty," says my grandma. She's talking about the soup. Which she has finished.

"Sorry, Mom," says my mother.

"A girl at school is pregnant," I say. To no one in particular.

"Oh?" says my mother.

"Yeah," I say. "I guess she must have let herself get too passionate."

"I guess," says my father, digging into his soup.

"Yeah," I say. "I guess that's real easy to do. I mean, once you get . . . you know."

"Passionate?" my mother guesses.

"Yeah," I say. "I mean, once you get passionate, at all, it's probably hard not to just get more and more passionate, until . . . don't you think?"

My father mutters something into his soup.

"I mean, if you don't let yourself get passionate at all," I tell them, "then you never have to worry about getting pregnant at all. So, maybe that's the best thing to do —never let yourself get passionate."

"I don't think so," says my father.

"No," says my mother.

"Good soup," says my father.

"Is everyone finished?" says my mother.

"Help me clear?" she asks.

"Sure," I say.

"Is Grandma going too?" I ask.

"Of course," my mother whinnies.

There *is* a gift horse in my dining room.

It's a sign.

Just what I needed.

Seventeen ─────────────────────

I decide to call Caroline after all.

I call from my room. I tell Caroline my problem.

Michael.

Age—seventeen.

Sex appeal—seventeen million.

Estimated time of arrival—tomorrow afternoon.

And Saturday night. Maybe.

I am waffling.

What am I to do?

"Oh," says Caroline, a mouth full of hard candies. *"I thought he was sixteen!* Fifteen, maybe. Seventeen?"

"I counted his teeth," I tell her.

"How much faster do girls mature than boys?"

"A year or two," I guess.

"Is Michael immature?" she asks.

"Are you?" I snap.

"I am just trying to get you closer together," she snaps right back.

"I know," I tell her. "I'm sorry."

"Are you scared?" she asks.

"Of what?" I ask her.

"Messing around," she whispers.

"Yeah," I confess.

"Where you going?" she asks.

"To the movies," I tell her.

Michael asked me to the movies. To see *Mandingo.* Which is something like *Eden in Flames.*

"Oh-oh!" says Caroline.

"What do you think?" I ask her.

"Well," says Caroline, stretching it out, "I'd . . . I'd go out with him."

That's not what I need to know.

"About messing around?" she, the notorious hip-kisser, asks.

"Yeah," I say.

"Follow your heart," she says. "But not too far, you know?"

"Yeah," I tell her.

"That's what I'd do," she says.

"You'd mess around, but you wouldn't *mess around*?"

"Yeah," she says, "except—"

Crunch!

It's those hard candies.

"Caroline?"

"I've got a cavity!" she crows.

"Great!" I say.

"I've gotta tell my mother!" she yelps.

Watch out, Dr. Donnie!

"Sure," I say. "Nice going!"

"Bye, Jessie," she says.

And we hang up.

With everything settled.

I decide to practice my guitar.

For tomorrow's lesson.

I might as well be prepared for whatever I can get prepared for.

E major 7th.

A major 7th.

F# major 7th.

B 7th.

After a while, there's a knock at my door.

"Yeah?" I say.

"Jessie."

It's Grandma!

Now, Grandma has mellowed out since she went to Israel, but I don't think she's ever been in my room.

I jump off my bed—where I've been practicing—and clear off the chair.

Except, while I'm clearing off the chair, Grandma sits down on my bed.

"Come," she says. "Jessie, come."

So I go to the bed and sit next to her.

And she puts her arm around me.

"So," she says. "Boys."

Which is a knockout. I mean, she really doesn't miss a thing.

"Always boys," she says. "Even Grandma."

"Grandpa," I say.

"No," she says.

"In Russia?" I ask.

She smiles and nods her head and hugs me closer.

"Who was he?" I ask.

"A boy," she says.

"Sweet," she says.

"Like sugar," she says. "Strong . . . tall . . . I was a girl."

"How old?"

"Thirteen," she says.

"What was his name?"

I see her remembering. Remembering herself. Remembering.

"Duvid," she says.

"Duvid," I say. It sounds so romantic. Duvid.

"So strong," she says, "so tall. My friend. My friend, all summer long."

And she is thirteen.

And she is in Russia.

And I can see her.

"Duvid, Duvid," she says, like she's calling him back to her from the past, her past, his past, "working in the fields. Oh, such hard work. You should never know. Never. But with my friend, Duvid, not so bad. Not so bad as before. Not so bad with Duvid . . . Everyone loved Duvid. He was on fire. Inside. You could see in his eyes. Fire. And all around him, it was warm."

Like Michael, I think. Michael's like that.

"I loved him, too," she says.

"I was a girl. Duvid was a man. . . . All the girls loved Duvid. All the women. All the men, too. And Duvid was loving with them all.

"But when Duvid said goodbye—he was going to his family in Palestine . . ."

I can see him, almost. Tall and strong and young. His

suitcase—probably one of those old ones with the belts to hold them together—his suitcase is in his hand. He's saying goodbye to the people on the farm, where the fields are.

I can see my grandma—only thirteen—standing with all the people, saying goodbye to Duvid, who they all loved, who they'll all miss.

"So, when he said goodbye to all of them, he came to me. In front of all of them, Duvid came to me. And, 'Esther,' he said—loud enough so everybody could hear —'Esther,' he said, 'I will miss you most of all.' "

"Oh, Grandma!"

"And Duvid kissed me.

"And then he went, my Duvid.

"My Duvid, my Duvid."

My grandmother is crying and rocking and remembering Duvid—for me—she's doing it for me.

She wants me to know.

About love.

About passion.

I didn't invent them.

She knows about them, too.

She knew about them when she was thirteen.

In Russia.

So, they must be all right.

Even if you're thirteen.

In Englewood, New Jersey.

Love and passion are all right.

"Thank you, Grandma," I tell her.

I throw my arms around her and, suddenly, I'm crying too.

"Thank you, Grandma."

"Jessie," she says, kissing me. "Jessie."

Eighteen _____

I've decided.

I can't decide.

Until I see how things go at the lesson.

When I see how things go—how I feel, how Michael acts—I'll decide.

So, how are things going?

Great.

I mean the lesson's going fine.

We're sitting on chairs, opposite each other. Michael and I. We've got our feet up on chairs, next to each other. Our guitars are in our laps.

First Michael plays something—some new combination of the four chords—and then I try it. As soon as I get it right, Michael smiles and nods and throws a new combination at me.

We've been doing this for almost an hour now, and I've been sticking with Michael pretty well. I can tell that he's impressed with my progress and that he's having a good time.

I'm having a good time, too. For one thing, I've hardly even thought about Saturday night, the whole time.

So, I finish up playing this fairly difficult thing Michael gave me. And he smiles and nods and starts this really complicated kind of strumming.

"Hey!" I say. "That's not fair!"

"I know," he smiles, "but I've got another lesson at five-thirty."

"Oh," I say. And I stand up, fast.

I can't put it off much longer.

I head for my guitar case, by the door.

Saturday night is going to have to be dealt with.

"So," says Michael, a second later. He's standing right behind me. I'm putting my guitar case away, and Michael's standing right behind me. "So," he says. "Saturday night?"

I nod my head.

"Great!" says Michael.

And you can see his eyes relax and shine, like I've just given him a very nice present.

"Mandingo?" he says.

"Mandingo," I answer.

I'm actually going through with it.

"Pick you up around seven?" he asks.

"Uh . . . no . . . seven-thirty, okay?"

"Okay, Jess," he says. And he looks at me. Looks into my eyes. And he reaches out his hand, and touches my hair.

I feel my body—my breath, coming fast; my heart, pounding in my chest.

I know I've made a terrible mistake.

"Michael—"

Bang!

She walks through the door.

"Whoops," she says.

"Sorry," she says.

And I'm back on Earth.

And the chance is gone.

"That's okay," Michael tells the girl.

He's dropped his hand from my hair.

I finish up my packing.

"You sure?" she asks. "I mean, I can wait."

"I gotta go," I say. "Thanks for the lesson, Michael."

And I bolt for the door.

I am halfway down the corridor, when I hear Michael call, "Bye!"

"Bye," I shout.

"See you tomorrow," I say. I say it too quietly for anybody to hear.

I just want to remind myself.

I could tie a string around my finger.

Or a rope around my neck.
Just to remind myself, of course.
What have I done?
What am I going to do?

Nineteen ———————

First, my father can't tie his tie.

You have to wear a tuxedo to this wedding and you have to wear a bow tie with it and my father can't tie his bow tie.

And it's seven o'clock, Saturday night, and Michael's due in half an hour and I'm not dressed or anything because, as far as my parents are concerned, I'm going over to Caroline's and you don't get dressed to go over to Caroline's.

"It's getting late," I remind my father.

My mother is almost made up and everything but dressed. She's at her vanity table, putting the finishing touches on her eyes.

"Never fear," my father tells me. "Bob Walters can get the job done."

"I hope so," I tell him.

"Never fear," he says.

And he goes over to his closet and he takes his bow tie off!

Great.

"Attendez!" he says. It's French for "Watch!"

He comes out of his closet with this bow tie in his hand, only it's already tied, and *snap-snap*, my father's dressed!

"Voilà!" he says. It's French for "Ta-dah!"

My mother, sitting at her vanity, laughs and claps her hands.

"Poetry in motion," she tells my father. And she gets up from her vanity and walks over toward the bathroom, where her dress is hanging.

107

"Not so bad yourself," says my father, watching her walk.

She's got a nice walk, my mother.

I think I got mine from her.

So my mother turns and gives my father a smile and a wink, as she disappears into the bathroom.

And my grandma comes in.

"Grandma's ready," I shout to my mother.

"Good," she shouts back.

"Esther!" says my father, turning to my grandma, acting like he's really knocked out by how terrific she looks.

She does look pretty terrific.

And my father starts waltzing over to her—I swear!—waltzing and singing this song!

It is five after seven!

"Mom!" I call to my mother.

My father takes my grandmother in his arms and the two of them are dancing.

It's almost six after seven and they're dancing!

"Mom!"

"Yes," she says. And she comes out of the bathroom. Dressed.

"Mo-om!" I say. She looks great.

"Lois!" says my father. "You look fantastic!"

And he leaves my grandma and goes over and kisses my mother.

And my grandma takes off for the door!

"Where you going, Grandma?!" I shout and I run across the bed and head her off at the door.

"I have to change," she says.

"No! Why? You look terrific!" I tell her. "Doesn't she, Mom? Dad?"

"You look fine," says my mother.

"Elegant," says my father.

"Too dark," says my grandma, shaking her head.

"Really, Grandma!" I tell her. "You look very pretty. And it's *late*," I add.

"It is," says my father.

"Grandma?" I say. And I'm *pleading* with her.

"Well," she says.

And then she smiles. And she pinches my cheek.

Which means it's okay. She won't change.

So everybody's dressed.

And down the stairs.

And at the front door.

I see them out.

I say goodnight to my father.

I tell my grandma to have a good time.

My mother tells me to have a good time, too, and "Don't stay too late at Caroline's," she says.

I tell her I won't.

She hugs me.

I feel like a rat.

And they're gone.

It is ten after seven.

I have just twenty minutes to shower and wash my hair and blow it dry and put it up. Michael's never seen my hair up. I look older with my hair up.

I also have to dress. In my dusty-rose off-the-shoulders lace top. And my tiered-cotton white skirt. And my dusty-rose espadrilles that lace up around my calves. And the necklace Grandma gave me, with the rose and ruby-colored stones. And my little gold earrings. Heart-shaped.

And makeup, of course. For luck. And courage.

I have just twenty minutes.

I do it in nineteen, flat.

A new world's record.

It is seven-twenty-nine, exactly.

And I have nothing to do but wait.

Wait for Michael.

And calm myself.

I wait on the stairs by the front door. Just opposite the clock.

I close my eyes and practice breathing calmly. In. Out. In. Out.

If you concentrate on it—and don't think about Michael—you can do it.

I can do it!

I'm doing it.

Breathing calmly.

And I hear a car, coming. Getting closer.

But it goes past.

In. Out. In. Out.

Another car is coming.

Closer!

It's stopping!

I hear the car door slam! I hear his footsteps, coming up the walk! Onto the porch! He's at the door!

It's Michael.

I am not afraid.

I am petrified!

Twenty ————————————

There has been a slight misunderstanding.

I realize this as we are driving to the movies. Michael and I, side by side on the front seat of his station wagon, getting along fine, so far, pretty relaxed, pretty easy.

Until Michael makes a wrong turn.

"I thought *Mandingo* was at the Park Hill," I say.

That's the theater in downtown Englewood.

"Could be," Michael says, "but I know for sure it's at the Starlight."

"Oh," I say.

The Starlight's a drive-in!

"Music?" says Michael.

"Huh?" I say.

"Oh," I say, "sure."

Michael turns on the radio and drives to the Starlight.

I pretend it isn't happening.

I mean, I pretend we're not driving into a drive-in theater.

I pretend we're not in the refreshment stand, loading up on snacks and drinks.

I pretend we're not back in the car, eating and drinking and listening to the radio and waiting for the show to start.

I even pretend we're not having this little conversation straight through all of this stuff I *know* isn't happening.

It works fine.

Right up until the movie starts.

When the movie starts, the pretending stops.

I am at this drive-in with Michael.

Sooner or later, he's going to kiss me, and I'm going to kiss him back.

And he's going to kiss me, again. And I'm going to kiss him back, again.

And he's going to want to be closer to me. And I'm going to want to be closer to him.

And he'll get closer.

And I'll get closer.

And it won't be close enough.

Not for him.

Not for me.

And then.

And then.

And—

I don't want to think about it!

But you have to.

I have to.

I'm thirteen!

If I was sixteen, I'd have probably been through this already, and I'd know!

I mean, I know a little about sex.

The technical side of it.

What goes where.

How not to get pregnant.

What I don't know is all the rest of it.

This is all the rest of it!

Or it will be.

If I don't confess.

Tell Michael everything.

Now.

Before it starts.

That's what I should do.

"Root beer?" says Michael.

Mandingo is up on the screen and squawking out of the loudspeaker on the car window, and Michael's offering me a root beer.

I have to tell him now.

"I'm not finished," I tell him. I am nearing the bottom of a box of popcorn.

"Here's looking at you, sweetheart."

I give him my very worst Bogart imitation, toast him with my popcorn, throw my head back and empty the last kernels into my mouth.

"Michael," I begin.

112

It comes out soft.

Too soft for Michael to hear.

He's singing to himself.

"She's still a mys-ter-y to me . . ." he sings.

"What's that?" I ask him.

"Oh," he says, "that's John Sebastian."

I don't know him.

"He wrote a lot of good things," Michael says, "like . . ."
And he sings,

A younger girl keeps rollin' cross my mi-ind . . .

"Oh, Michael!" I say.

Only it's a sob.

And all of a sudden I'm crying.

And I'll never be able to stop.

"What's wrong, Jess?" he asks. "Something's been wrong all night."

My face is streaked with tears. I don't want him to see me cry. But what does it matter?

I turn to Michael.

"Can I kiss you?" he says.

"Please." I mean "No," but I say "Please."

Michael doesn't understand.

He thinks I'm telling him to ask me more politely.

"Please?" he says.

And he leans toward me, his eyes on my eyes, until the last second, and then, darkness—his lips on my lips, his mouth, Michael.

And I am gone, spinning, swirling, lost and falling, falling, falling slowly down.

And I settle.

And I look.

And I see Michael.

Next to me.

We are lying on the seat, next to each other. Michael is propped up on his elbow, looking down at me. My head is resting in his hand.

"I like you a lot, Jess," he says.

"I like you, too, Michael," I say.

"No," I say, "it's worse than that.

"I love you, Michael," I say.

"Jess!" he says, surprised.

"From the first time I saw you," I tell him, "at the shopping mall."

"Shopping mall?" he says. And he lifts up on his elbow, thinking. Puzzled. Just the trace of a smile on his face.

"In Lodi?" he says.

He remembers!

"We don't play a lot of shopping malls," he says.

He doesn't remember.

"Lodi," he says. "Lodi . . . sure. Sure!"

And he starts singing.

> *It's better than it's ever been,*
> *Better than it's ever been . . .*

And I join in.

> *Better than it's ever been before.*

"You're her!"

He remembers!

"The girl at the mall!" he says. "Down front, on the right."

"Oh, Michael!" I'm crying, again.

I have to tell him!

"Please," I say.

And I turn my head away.

"I don't get it," says Michael.

"I know," I say. And I sit up.

And I straighten my skirt.

"Tell me!"

"It's because I liked you," I tell him.

And here it comes.

"And I wanted you to like me!" I say.

"And I knew it would be impossible, unless I lied!

"And I didn't see why it *should* be impossible, but it is."

"Because I'm not Catholic?" he says.

"I'm not Catholic," I tell him.

"What?"

"I'm Jewish."

"Oh," he says. But he's confused. "So what?" he says.

"That's not it," I tell him.

114

"What *is* it, Jessie?!"

He's shouting.

"Are you . . . dying of leukemia or what?" he says.

"I'm thirteen."

He makes a sound, like I punched him in the stomach.

He looks like I've slapped his face.

"I'll be sixteen two years from next June fourteenth," I tell him.

But he doesn't hear me.

He's starting the car.

We're going.

Nowhere.

I can cry, now.

Twenty-one _____

I cry all the way home from the drive-in. To myself. I don't cry out loud.

Michael doesn't speak, and I don't try.

What is there to say?

I cry until we pull up to my house.

"Bye, Jessie."

"I love you, Michael."

"Do you think that helps?"

"I didn't mean to . . . to be a tease."

"Bye, Jessie."

"Bye, Michael."

I cry from the second Michael pulls away in his car until my parents come home from the wedding. About five hours off and on. Mostly on.

I also eat a whole Sara Lee chocolate cake.

Sunday I am sick all day. I am pale and sick to my stomach and feverish, although I don't have a temperature.

And I don't feel much like eating or talking to anyone or being with anyone.

Monday is school, and even though I still feel sick, my mother's not going to let me out of it. She's a teacher, and I'm going.

I'm at the breakfast table in the kitchen, pushing my cereal around the bottom of the bowl.

"I'm going to take my car in today," says my mother to my father.

"Oh?" he says.

"I've got some errands to run at lunchtime," my mother explains.

He finishes his coffee and gets up from the table. He

says goodbye to my mother and kisses her, like he always does.

"Bye, Jess," he says to me.

"Have a nice day," I tell him. I say it halfheartedly, not looking up from my cereal bowl.

"What it lacks in originality," he says, "it makes up for in sincerity."

"Sorry," I say. "Have a—" I catch myself. I'm embarrassed. I say, "See you tonight."

"I'll bring you a chocolate Easter bunny," he says.

"Yeah?" I say.

He knows they're my favorite.

"Yeah," he says. "Remind me when it's Easter."

I laugh. Kind of.

And he kisses me. Really. Like he always does.

And he goes out the back door and gets into his car and drives out the driveway and heads off to work.

My mother and I don't talk until he's gone.

"I don't have any errands to run at lunchtime," my mother says.

"I didn't think so," I tell her, still messing around with my cereal.

"Jessie," she says, "if you look at me—I promise you—you won't turn into a pillar of salt."

I look at her.

"See?" she says.

I freeze.

Like in statue tag.

"I spoke too soon," she gasps.

It's an old joke between us.

Nobody says anything for a second.

"Is it a boy?"

"It *was*," I tell her.

Then she gets up from the table and carries her coffee cup and my father's coffee cup over to the sink.

"How come you never told me?" she asks. She's more curious than she is angry. But she's angry, too.

"There wasn't anything to tell," I tell her. And I get up and carry my cereal bowl over to the sink.

"Not really," I say.

We are both standing there by the sink. I'm having a

118

hard time looking at my mother. Looking her in the eye. I'm looking at her shoes instead.

"He's the first boy you've . . . dated?" she asks. Very even. Very controlled.

"We went to a movie," I tell her.

"Saturday night?" she says. She's surprised. And maybe she's getting a little angrier now.

"Yes."

"Did you think I wouldn't let you?" she asks. She can't quite believe I'd lie to her.

She's looking for a reason.

"Nothing happened," I tell her.

"You lied to me," she says. "That happened."

"Just stupid, I guess. I'm sorry."

And I am. Sorry enough to cry.

"I just wish I'd known," she says. "There are things," she says, "things we should talk about."

"I know about the medical part," I tell her.

I can see the relief on her face.

"And the heart part?" she asks.

I can't hold it back anymore.

She takes me in her arms and holds me.

"That's the hardest part," she says.

And then she holds me a little away from her, and she looks me in the eye. She's crying too.

"But you wouldn't want to miss it," she says.

"No," I tell her.

"Even," she says, "even if, sometimes——"

"Yeah," I say, "even if."

"It's worth it," she says. "Honest."

I see she means it. I've seen her live it. And I believe it's true.

"I know," I tell her.

And it's a sob.

And I'm in her arms again.

"It's so hard, Mom. Why is it so hard?"

"I wish I could tell you, Jess. But I can't. I don't know the answer. I wish I did."

We have a pretty good cry together, the two of us, my mother and me, standing in the kitchen, by the sink.

And before long, we've kind of cried ourselves out.

"How do you like being a grown-up, so far?" she says.

"Not much," I tell her.

And she laughs.

"It gets better," she says.

"You promise?" I ask her.

"Promise," she says.

And she gives me one last hug.

"Ready for school?"

"Yeah," I say, "ready as I'll ever be."

On the way to school—she drives me—I tell her about Michael. She's real nice about it. Considering.

It doesn't help.

Twenty-two ─────────────────

The way to get back to leading a normal life, everyone says, is by *leading* a normal life. Whether you feel like it or not.

That makes sense to me.

But it takes concentration.

Which I don't have.

All through the day at school, I can't think of anything but Michael and what I've done to him and how he must be feeling.

He was so mad.

Because I lied to him.

But more because he believed in my lie.

More because I made him feel like a jerk.

I did that.

And so he's mad at me.

He was disappointed, too.

Disappointed in me, for playing games with people's feelings.

I did that, too.

And he was hurt.

And that's the worst part.

He let himself like me.

And now, he's kicking himself for letting himself like me.

And I did that.

To Michael.

Saturday night.

And it's Monday afternoon.

And school's out.

And the way to get back to leading a normal life, every-one says, is by leading a normal life.

I'm in Hackensack.

Downtown Hackensack.

My feet know the way, so I follow them.

In the door, up the stairs, through the door.

Michael's not in today.

"Here," says Eddie Nova, "the pinky goes here."

I strum the chord he's teaching me.

Maybe two octopuses could play it. I sure can't.

"No," says Eddie, "when you put your pinky here, you gotta keep your pointer there."

"Oh," I say.

But my pinky's already forgotten where here is and my pointer can't reach to there.

I strum.

Eddie winces.

"No wonder Michael's playing hooky," he says.

"I thought he was sick!"

"Nah!" he says. "Michael doesn't get sick. He's a Christian Science kind of kid. No. Michael gets bored. Michael gets impatient. He's young. I'm used to it. Play."

I strum.

Eddie winces.

"Good," he says. "Keep at it. I gotta make a call."

He gets up from the chair across from me and heads for the door.

"Right back," he says.

He shouldn't have given me such a hard chord.

He should have given me something maybe just a bit harder than the chords I already know.

E major 7th.

E major 7th.

A major 7th.

A major 7th.

F# major 7th.

F# major 7th.

B 7th.

B 7th.

They sound so pretty as I strum them.

Someone has painted a pair of boots on the rug in front

of me. I catch them out of the corner of my eye, while I'm strumming.

I don't look at them directly. I keep them in the corner of my eye and keep strumming.

Out of the corner of my eye, these boots someone's painted on the rug look very real. In fact, they look very like Michael's boots. Which is probably because I am looking at them out of the corner of my eye.

If I really looked at them, I know these boots someone's painted on the rug would just turn into a shadow, cast by a chair sitting at a funny angle in front of the window.

I look at the boots.

They *are* boots.

Michael's boots!

"Michael!"

He's in his boots!

They aren't painted on the rug!

He's here!

Or is he?

He doesn't speak.

He doesn't say a word.

He just stares at me.

Like a statue.

But no.

He moves.

He turns and walks away and puts his guitar case on the piano bench and opens it and lifts out his guitar and starts playing.

The four chords.

The ones he taught me.

Still strumming, he turns and faces me. Except he doesn't look at me. His eyes are on his guitar, as he walks over and stands in front of me.

I am so sorry!

I am so sorry, Michael!

I join in, playing along with Michael.

It's to say I'm sorry.

And I understand.

And he doesn't have to talk to me.

He doesn't have to look at me.

Because I know what a lousy thing I've done to him. And any way he wants to feel about me—any way he wants to act toward me—I've got it coming and it's all right.

I try to put all this into the four chords I'm playing. I try to put it all into the four chords.

It's impossible, I know.

But Michael hears it.

He looks up at me.

He lifts his eyes from his guitar and looks into my eyes.

"I'm used to older women," he says.

He says it like he's just picking up the conversation where we left off.

"I'm used to spin-the-bottle," I tell him.

"Really?" he says.

And it's funny to him. Like he can't believe it.

"Yeah," I tell him.

Michael smiles and shakes his head.

"I've never *done* anything like—"

"I know," he says.

"Could . . . could you tell?!"

He smiles. And shakes his head.

"We'd have to go real slow," he says.

Which stops me.

Stops my strumming.

My breathing.

Everything.

No.

Not this time.

Michael's giving me a second chance.

"Could we?" I ask him. *"Could* we go slow?"

Michael's stopped strumming. He's just standing there. Looking at me. Thinking.

He shakes his head.

"I don't know," he says.

And he sighs.

And he drops his eyes to his guitar.

And he strums.

The four chords.

"Michael?"

He looks up from his guitar.

"Would you kiss me?"

He looks puzzled.

"Now?"

124

He stops strumming.

"Please?"

Michael kisses me.

Just barely.

So lingeringly.

So good!

And then he stands up, away from me.

"Well?" he says.

"I don't know either," I tell him.

I don't know.

And Michael doesn't know.

We strum our guitars.

I wish I was either a little girl or a woman.

I wish I wasn't in between.

I wish, if I had to be in between, Michael would be in between, too.

But I know the world isn't made of wishes. Not mine, anyway. And Michael is so many wishes come true.

"It'd be up to you," he says. "Setting the pace. Saying yes. Saying no."

"Would you listen?"

Michael looks at me. Looks into my eyes. Looks as deep as he can see. As deep as I can show him.

But the answer isn't there.

"I'd try," he says.

"Would you? Really?"

"I love you too, Jess."

"Michael!"

"And besides," he says—he smiles and shrugs his shoulders—"you picked up the *guitar* pretty quick, so—"

"Michael!" I say. I say it like "How dare you!"

"Put a finish on it, Jess," he says.

And I can tell by the way he's smiling at me he doesn't want me to play the B 7th chord.

I know Michael wants me in his arms.

And so, I stand.

And I go to him.

And he opens his arms.

And takes me in. . . .

AVON ◮ CONTEMPORARY READING FOR YOUNG PEOPLE

- ☐ **Pictures That Storm Inside My Head**
  Richard Peck, ed.   43489 $1.50

- ☐ **Don't Look and It Won't Hurt**
  Richard Peck   45120 $1.50

- ☐ **Through a Brief Darkness**
  Richard Peck   42093 $1.50

- ☐ **Go Ask Alice**   51730 $1.95

- ☐ **A Hero Ain't Nothin' but a Sandwich**
  Alice Childress   33423 $1.50

- ☐ **It's Not What You Expect**   Norma Klein   43455 $1.50

- ☐ **Mom, the Wolfman and Me**
  Norma Klein   49502 $1.75

- ☐ **Johnny May**   Robbie Branscum   28951 $1.25

- ☐ **Blackbriar**   William Sleator   30247 $1.25

- ☐ **Run**   William Sleator   45302 $1.50

- ☐ **Soul Brothers and Sister Lou**
  Kristin Hunter   42143 $1.50

- ☐ **A Teacup Full of Roses**
  Sharon Bell Mathis   49759 $1.50

- ☐ **An American Girl**   Patricia Dizenzo   51813 $1.95

**Where better paperbacks are sold or directly from the publisher.
Include 50¢ per copy for postage and handling; allow 4-6 weeks for delivery.**

Avon Books, Mail Order Dept.
224 West 57th Street, New York, N.Y. 10019

CR 8-80

AVON ◆ CONTEMPORARY READING
FOR YOUNG PEOPLE

☐ **Fox Running** R. R. Knudson	43760	$1.50
☐ **The Cay** Theodore Taylor	51037	$1.75
☐ **The Owl's Song** Janet Campbell Hale	28738	$1.25
☐ **The House of Stairs** William Sleator	32888	$1.25
☐ **Listen for the Fig Tree** Sharon Bell Mathis	51854	$1.95
☐ **Me and Jim Luke** Robbie Branscum	52688	$1.75
☐ **None of the Above** Rosemary Wells	26526	$1.25
☐ **Representing Superdoll** Richard Peck	47845	$1.75
☐ **Some Things Fierce and Fatal** Joan Kahn, ed.	32771	$1.50
☐ **The Sound of Chariots** Mollie Hunter	26658	$1.25
☐ **Guests in the Promised Land** Kristin Hunter	27300	$ .95
☐ **Taking Sides** Norma Klein	41244	$1.50
☐ **Sunshine** Norma Klein	76307	$2.25
☐ **Why Me? The Story of Jennie** Patricia Dizenzo	76331	$1.95
☐ **Forgotten Beasts of Eld** Patricia McKillip	42523	$1.75

Where better paperbacks are sold or directly from the publisher.
Include 50¢ per copy for postage and handling; allow 4-6 weeks for
delivery.

Avon Books, Mail Order Dept.
224 West 57th Street, New York, N.Y. 10019

CRY 8-80